ANATOMY
of a
MISFIT

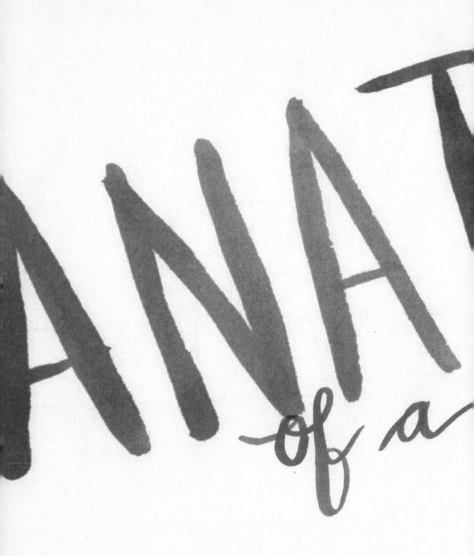

ANAT... of a

HARPER TEEN
An Imprint of HarperCollinsPublishers

OMY

MISFIT

Andrea Portes

HarperTeen is an imprint of HarperCollins Publishers.

Anatomy of a Misfit

Library of Congress Cataloging-in-Publication Data
Portes, Andrea.
Anatomy of a misfit / Andrea Portes. — First edition
pages cm
Summary: "The third most popular girl in school's choice between the hottest boy in town
and a lonely but romantic misfit ends in tragedy and self-realization"— Provided by publisher.
ISBN 978-0-06-231364-5 (hardback) — ISBN 978-0-06-236677-1 (int. ed.)
[1. Popularity—Fiction. 2. Dating (Social customs)—Fiction. 3. High schools—Fiction.
4. Schools—Fiction.] I. Title.
PZ7.P83615An 2014   2014008722
[Fic]—dc23   CIP
AC

Typography by Ellice M. Lee
14 15 16 17 18   CG/RRDH   10 9 8 7 6 5 4 3 2 1
❖
First Edition

For Dylan

This is a novel based on my ninth-grade year of junior high. I wrote this story because I wish I could go back in time and give this message to myself.

one

Pedaling fast fast fast, this is the moment. One of those movie moments you never think is gonna happen to you, but then it happens to you, and now it's here.

Pedaling fast fast fast, this is my only chance to stop it. This is the place where it looks like everything is gonna go horribly wrong and there's no hope, but then because it's a movie there is hope after all and there is a surprise that changes everything and everyone breathes a sigh of relief and everybody gets to go home and feel good about themselves and maybe fall asleep in the car.

Pedaling fast fast fast, this is the moment, this is the moment I get to remember for the rest of my nights and my days and my looking at the ceiling. Over that hill and down the next, through those trees and past the school.

Pedaling fast fast fast, this is the moment, by the time I get there you can see the lights going blue, red, white, blue, red, white, blue, red, white, little circles diced up in sirens and you think you can stop it but of course you can't, how could you ever think you could?

Pedaling fast fast fast, this is the moment.

This is the moment, and it's too late.

two

You're never gonna believe what happened. Okay. Let's just start from the beginning.

Logan McDonough's dad bought him a moped. That was the first thing.

Let's say Logan had showed up first thing, first day of school, tenth grade, at Pound High School, Lincoln, Nebraska, having never ever set foot here before, on his black moped, in his black mod outfit, with his black mod haircut. He woulda been a hit. Even Becky Vilhauer, aka number one most popular girl in the school, aka Darth Vader, woulda swooned.

But he had been here before, in ninth grade. When he was a nerd.

So you can see how his actions were totally illegal.

You can't just decide somewhere between May and August that you are going to change your whole identity, jump from geek to cool kid, get a jet-black haircut, peg your jet-black jeans, lose twenty pounds, and drive a Vespa. No way. That is totally against the rules and everybody knows it.

The audacity! Becky Vilhauer was not having it. I know, because she was right there next to me when he pulled up to school and you shoulda seen her jaw drop. She was *pissed*.

If you're wondering what I was doing standing right there next to Becky, aka the dark side of the force, it's because I am number three in the pecking order around here. I have no hope for rising above my station and I will explain why later. But number three is where I will always be and, as I am constantly reminded, I am lucky to be here.

Between number one and number three is Shelli Schroeder. Number two. She's my best friend even though she's kind of a slut. She told me something I immediately wanted to unhear and now I'm gonna tell you and you too will immediately want to unhear it. She makes out and even does the old in-and-out with the high school rockers. Like a lot. One time she told me Rusty Beck told her she has "the biggest pussy he's ever fucked." Yup. Try to unhear that. Nosiree, you cannot. By the way, she told me this like it was a compliment. I didn't have the heart to tell her I'm pretty sure that wasn't going to get her a date to the prom.

I like Shelli but it's kinda weird how she draws on her eyeliner. She kind of just circles both her eyes so you just get these two black almonds staring at you all the time. Imploringly. There's definitely something about Shelli's look that makes you feel like you're always supposed to help her out in some way. I guess that's why those rocker guys are always helping her out of her clothes.

Okay, so the reason why I'm number three and can never even hope to dream of being number two or number one is because my dad is Romanian and looks like Count Chocula. Seriously. He looks like a vampire. Never mind that we never see him and that he lives half the time in Princeton and half the time in Romania. That doesn't matter. All that matters is that he left me with a weird last name: Dragomir. And, to seal the deal, an even weirder first name: Anika.

Anika Dragomir.

So, you see, there is no hope.

You try going to a school of Jennys and Sherris and Julies with a name like Anika Dragomir.

Go ahead. I dare you.

But right now, that's not the story. Right now, no one can believe how Logan drives up to the front school steps.

Like a total. Baller.

And even better, he doesn't even acknowledge Becky

Vilhauer when she scoffs at him on his new moped.

"So, what? Now he's a nerd on wheels?"

And this is what's so weird about the whole thing: Even Shelli notices, which she tells me later on our endless, seriously endless, like we-should-be-put-in-child-protective-services endless, walk home from school. Logan doesn't notice what Becky says because he's not even looking at Becky. And he's not looking at Shelli, either. No, no.

Logan McDonough—nerd-ball turned goth-romance hero—is looking directly, and only, at *me*.

three

By the time I get home my stupid sisters are already locked in their room listening to the Stones and talking on the phone to more boys who don't like them. My brothers are in the back, probably setting fire to themselves or killing something.

In case you're wondering about the pecking order around here, it goes like this: My oldest sister, Lizzie, the leader of the pack, is the one who looks, dresses, and acts like Joan Jett and teases me endlessly for having boobs 'cause she is flat as a board, so fuck her. The second oldest is Neener, she kinda looks like Bambi and as far as I can tell her only distinguishing quality is she likes strawberries. Next up is Robby, he's the happy-go-lucky one everybody likes and never has any problems and looks all bright eyed and cute, like the Gerber baby. Then there's my other brother, Henry, who looks like Peter Brady and has been brooding ever since he was three. And then, last but not least, there's me. I'm the youngest and the one that everyone has decided is mentally deranged.

They're wrong, of course, but I don't mind letting them think that, because everyone lives in constant fear I'm going to kill myself and that's alright with me.

I bet you think I have dark hair and dark eyes and look like I listen to the Cure but you're wrong. On the outside I look like vanilla pudding so nobody knows that on the inside I am spider soup.

Unless they look closer.

For instance . . . Yes, there is blonde hair, blue eyes, pale skin. That is true. But, you see . . . everybody around here has a button nose and I have more of a nose that looks like it got lopped off by a meat cleaver. There's another thing, too—I have a boy jaw, like a square jaw, and cheekbones you could cut yourself on. Also, there are dark purple circles around my eyes that might be adorable if I was a raccoon. So, you see, I'm hideous. Also, there is the fact that Becky constantly calls me "immigrant." That doesn't exactly help.

And yet . . . If you don't look close enough, you would never know I'm not made of apple pie. You have to truly inspect me to see that I am obviously from a place where

Vlad the Impaler is everybody's great-great-grandfather and you have to survive on one turnip a week, which you have split with your brothers and three cousins who live in the attic.

But this is not a complete liability. In fact, it's probably why, two years back, I won that fight at the roller-skating rink. Here's what happened: Russ Kluck, from the wrong side of the tracks, liked me and kept trying to get me to couples skate with him. Even though everyone knows he lives in a trailer, everyone thought I should be flattered, but I don't really know how to talk to boys so I just sprayed ketchup all over him.

He thought that was cute and liked me even more but that just made this other wrong-side-of-the-tracks girl jealous. She liked Russ and couldn't believe I sprayed him with ketchup. I bet she thought she was getting into a fight with a vanilla wafer on roller skates but little did she know she was getting in a fight with a spider sandwich.

Look, I'm gonna explain my insect insides but you have to promise not to feel sorry for me, okay? This is not a sob story. These are just the facts. Plain and simple.

My dad, Count Chocula, basically kidnapped us and brought us with him to a castle in Romania when I was three. Maybe it was more like a chateau. Whatever, to a three-year-old, it felt like a castle. It was me, my real sister,

Lizzie, and my real brother, Henry, practically all alone in that castle, with Count Chocula gone half the time but that was okay because when he actually was there it was kind of like having a walking wraith eating your Cheerios with you. I'm serious, this guy could basically freeze the air just by strolling in the room. It's not like we ever did anything wrong, either. Are you kidding? We were too scared. It was obvious if we even spilled a drop of milk on the stone castle floor we would be encased in glass and sent into the phantom zone, never to return. Luckily, there was a nice nanny for a while. But he got her pregnant and she left.

My mom didn't have any way to get us back so it took me standing up to my dad when I was ten to finally get back home to her and her new husband. So, to recap, I was raised from three to ten by a wraithlike vampire in a freezing stone castle in Romania. Don't feel sorry for me, that's not what this is about. This is about spider stew.

Wrong-side-of-the-tracks girl didn't know what she was going up against at the roller-skating rink and I don't blame her. The legend goes that I pulled her hair out, dropped her to the ground, and kicked her repeatedly with my roller skate. But that's not what happened. It was more of a weird roller-skating dance—each of us pulling on each other and moving in a slow, deformed circle—that was ended by the manager. In all honesty, it was a draw. I guess that girl had a pretty tough rep, though, because nobody ever messed with me after that.

My sisters and brothers don't mess with me either, but that's because not only do they think I'm annoying and hate bringing me anywhere, but they are also worried I'm going to throw myself off the nearest bridge on their watch, in which case, they will be grounded for life.

Robby and Neener, my stepbrother and stepsister, are 100 percent purebred all-American. Their mom lives in a trailer next to a lake and there's even a horse. Also, a duck. Or so I'm told. They have no idea how lucky they are. I would give anything to have a dad who lived in a trailer instead of a castle, and maybe that sounds completely backward but you try growing up half vampire in Nebraska.

Henry, my real brother, doesn't care about being a half-breed because he knows once he graduates from Harvard and starts making a billion dollars no one will care and he can just buy all his friends at the friends store. And Lizzie. Well, Lizzie has decided to just go straight past half-breed, and full speed ahead into super-freak. She is dark. She is gamine. She is mean. She is Joan Jett. She will kill you. And you will know her by the trail of dead.

So, really, I'm the only one around here wrestling with an immigrant complex.

I bet you think I go to school with all these freaks but

I don't. Thank God. We live in this weird strip of suburb where you can choose either East High or Pound High. My sisters and brothers chose East High. So I chose Pound. I did this as a purely self-protective measure. My sisters, especially Lizzie, would have pursued, tortured, and harassed me endlessly if I set foot or even thought about setting foot near them. No, sir. High school would've become my own personal Spanish Inquisition crossed with Salem Witch Trials crossed with every movie you've ever seen with a marine sergeant torturing his underlings at boot camp. No thanks, folks. No way.

I cannot give Lizzie that pleasure.

Now, this brings us to my mom. Who is essentially the only decent one in the house. But if you think post-Chocula she went out and found the perfect husband, you can guess again. The guy she got is six foot three, three hundred pounds, and stands in front of us at the buffet line my mom sets out at dinner, eating all the food. If we are lucky we will get something good but you better grab it while you still have a chance. He never talks to us, except in grunts, and then goes straight to his room after dinner, to lie on his water bed and watch *Wheel of Fortune*.

So, basically, my real dad is a vampire and my stepdad is an ogre. If my mom gets married a third time it will clearly be to either a werewolf or a mummy. I'm sure she married this guy so her kids would have a home and all but, man oh man, I wish she could have found someone that made her happy.

I have an escape plan for Mom and me where we can leave all these jerkfaces in the dust, but I am only on stage 2 of that plan currently.

I'm looking at her in the kitchen and realizing that if you made a trajectory from Brigitte Bardot to Mrs. Santa Claus, my mom is one-third of the way from Brigitte Bardot over. She's a total dumpling about everything and certainly deserves better than this crap-hole.

"Honey, did anything exciting happen at your first day of school today?"

"Not really. Logan McDonough got a moped."

She's making Mexican casserole, which is heavy on the rotation and usually lands on a Monday night, unless there's gonna be Taco Tuesday.

"Oh, I bet that was a real hit."

"Not really. Becky told him he was a nerd on wheels."

"Well, that wasn't very nice of her."

"*Tsh*. Whatever. She's kind of a bitch."

"Honey, you know I don't like words like that."

"I know. She's just not very nice is all."

"Well, did you say something nice to him? I bet that woulda made his day."

"What?! No. Becky would kill me."

Now Mom stops putting the chips in the casserole and looks up. Real emphasis.

"You know what, honey, just because Becky does something doesn't mean you have to do it."

"Yeah, right. She's like the number one most popular girl, Mom."

"Well, why is that?"

"I dunno, she was like a model or something."

"A model?"

"Yeah."

"A model for what, might I ask, seeing as we live in this bastion of the fashion industry here in Lincoln, Nebraska?"

"I dunno. I think, like, the J. C. Penney catalog?"

"Oh, well that explains it."

"Mom, you just don't understand, okay?"

"Honey, all I'm saying is that you can stand up to her—"

"You mean like you do with Dad?"

But she doesn't take the bait. She just ignores me and puts the casserole in the oven instead. Doesn't matter, my brothers run in from the back and start tearing through the cupboards like the Four Horsemen of the Apocalypse are riding up from Kansas.

"Boys, now listen, it's only one hour to dinner. I don't want you to ruin your appetites."

Back in my room I get to flop down with no one around. One of the perks of being the youngest nobody likes? I get my own room. I had to share with Lizzie for a while but I just kept calling her a slut all night till she begged Mom to move her. Sounds mean, but the thing is, all she ever does is talk to boys all night on the phone and make it impossible to study. She blushes and giggles and then half the time sneaks out but I don't tell anyone because then I can use it to blackmail her. Now she's down with Neener and I get my whole room to decorate and think about how Logan lost twenty pounds and actually didn't look half bad.

four

My boss doesn't know I've been poisoning him.

Don't be jealous but Shelli and I got a job at the Bunza Hut. We get to wear lemon-colored fake polos, Kelly-green shorts, and banana LA Gear sneakers. We get to wear this every. Shift.

You have to stand back by the sundae machines, otherwise you'll be on camera the whole time and it's an invasion of privacy or whatever.

"Bubba thinks you're hard to get," Shelli says.

I snort. "I'm hard to get if your name's Bubba."

"They're having a party Friday. We should go."

"They're just gonna try to stick their wieners in us."

"You're such a prude."

"Wull, they are."

"Some girls actually like that kind of stuff."

"Like some girls named Shelli?"

Mr. Baum, who has absolutely no idea how high he is, pokes his head from the back.

"Am I paying you girls to drink milk shakes?"

You shoulda seen this guy before I started crunching up my mom's Valium and dosing his endless cup of Folger's. He was a total dick. Especially to Shelli. It was like that helpless, needy look in her almond-shaped eyes sparked something in him where he smelled blood. He tormented her. If she was sweeping, he'd say to mop. If she was mopping, he'd say to sweep. If she smiled at the customers, he'd say she was being too friendly. If she didn't smile, he'd say she wasn't being friendly enough. Black shoulda been white, white shoulda been black, and no matter what, she was an idiot. The guy's a sociopath. One day he made Shelli cry because he said her shorts needed to be pressed and she needed to lose ten pounds. That was the day I realized something had to be done.

So now I dose him. First thing after clocking in.

The trick is misdirection. You can't just crunch up Mom's Valium and put it in his mug. Are you crazy? He'd notice that in a second. You have to make small talk with a customer while doing the crunching. Of course, there is the issue of dosage.

Here's what happened the first time. About five weeks ago, the first Sunday of preseason football, Mr. Baum was hungover and it was practically an emergency because he was being a total jerkface.

He was nursing his headache in the back and I was up front chitchatting with a very nice family from Platte.

"Oh, those Huskers are looking good!"

Crunch. Crunch.

"Looks like this is gonna be our year."

Crunch. Crunch. Crunch.

"Those Sooners don't stand a chance!"

"Damn straight. Go Big Red!"

Pour the coffee in the mug.

Dose. Dose. Dose. Stir stir stir.

And then the happy Platte family makes their way to the table, Mr. Baum gets his Folger's, and everything is perfect.

Except.

Fifteen minutes later we hear a thud.

Shelli looks at me with her almond-eyes. There's no face anymore, just eyes.

I look at her and we both know the situation is dire.

"You go look."

"No, you."

"I can't go. You know how much he hates me. He'll kill me. If he's not already dead."

Shelli does have a point.

"Okay, what if we both go?"

"Like together?"

"Yeah, like together."

And now Shelli is holding my arm.

"Shelli, now's not the time to make a pass at me."

"Shut up!"

"I know I'm superhot but we have an emergency situation here."

I can't help it. It's too fun to tease Shelli. Also, she's a Christian, so if Mr. Baum is dead that means eternal damnation in the claws of the Beelzebub, whereas I will just be grounded.

By the time we make it into the back office there is nothing visible of Mr. Baum but his feet. He's wearing tassel shoes, which should be enough excuse for the poisoning, but the lack of movement here is certainly a cause for concern.

"Is he . . . is he . . . ?"

"If he is, Shelli, I really think you should keep your hands to yourself. It's important to respect the dead. Also, he might reawaken as a zombie."

"Shut up, Anika, God!"

"I also don't think you should take the Lord's name in vain in front of a zombie."

"Jesus!"

"That's the son of the Lord, Shelli. You just murdered someone and now you've taken the son of the Lord's name in vain."

"Anika, stop, seriously—"

"Look, there's no way he's dead."

"Are you sure?"

"Um, yeah."

"Smell him! He smells like a vodka plant."

"What, like a plant made of vodka?"

"No. Like a place where they make vodka. You know, like a rubber plant."

"Shelli, focus. I need you to check and see if he's dead."

"I'm not checking. You check."

"I can't. If I get closer he might bite me. We both know I'm Romanian and if I'm bit by the undead I will immediately become a vampire. Then, there's no chance for you."

"Well, I'm not getting cl—"

"*No chance*, Shelli! My ancient blood will overpower you. You'll probably just evaporate."

"I can't do it, Anika!" She's practically crying.

Mr. Baum's tassel shoes remain unmoved.

"Really the only solution is that we both look at the same time."

"Okay."

"Okay?"

"Yeah, okay."

Shelli grabs my arm and we go in closer, like two kittens investigating a fallen rhino.

We are almost to his comb-over when he snores so loud it throws us back into the other room.

Jesus.

That guy can snore!

"What do we do?! What do we do?!"

"Well, I dunno, Shelli. There's kind of two ways to look at it. Either . . . we tear ourselves apart with guilt that we are obviously horrible people or . . . OR . . . we accept that Mr. Baum is out for the day, make some sundaes, and prank phone call that hot new debate teacher."

"Seriously? Shouldn't we call someone?"

"Yeah, we should call that hot new debate teacher and ask him if he's heard that song by the Police about the '*young teacher, the subject, of schoolgirl fantasy . . .*'"

"You're crazy."

"Crazy for that debate teacher."

And that, ladies and gentlemen, is what happens when you are not paying attention to your Valium dose.

Since then, I have perfected my technique and we have had no further incidents. But as you can see, every cloud has a silver lining and, in this case, the silver lining is . . . ever since the Valium dosing has begun, Mr. Baum's behavior has much improved.

Like today. He's totally leaving us alone, probably sitting at his desk waving his fingers in front of his face and marveling over the psychedelic trails. But that's not important right now, what's important is that in my leisure time I have concocted a plan that I think might seriously upgrade our Halloween, Homecoming, and holiday season.

"I think I figured out how to steal from this place."

Shelli stops wiping the counters. Her eyes go wide. She really *does* look like a deer in headlights.

"Are you serious?"

"Yeah. Okay, so like . . . the camera's on the cash register, right?"

"Un-hunh."

"So we have to undercharge on the register but get the actual price from the customer, right?"

"I think so."

"Then just put all the money in the cash register, so the camera doesn't see anything, right?"

"Yeah?"

"But just keep a running tally, on the side, of the difference."

"I don't get it."

"Okay, like, say the Bunza meal is four dollars."

"Yeah?"

"So, we charge the customer four dollars, but we only ring up three on the cash register."

"Okay."

"But when you do that, like right when you do it, write down the difference."

"Okay."

"So, you write down a dollar, right?"

"I think so . . ."

"And then we just keep a running tally of the difference all day."

"Okay, then what?"

"Okay, so there's cameras everywhere, right?"

"Yeah."

"So, when we make the drop, at the end of the night, we gotta do it where there's no cameras, yeah?"

"Yeah . . ."

"So, where are there no cameras?"

"I dunno."

"Think."

"I dunno! You're stressing me out!"

"Shelli, I'm just trying to improve our lifestyle."

"Okay, well, just tell me, or . . . It's mean, it's like you're showing off or something."

"Okay. The answer is . . . there's no camera on . . . the stairs."

"What stairs?"

"The stairs down to the drop."

"Oh . . ."

"Think about it, it's perfect. All you do is take out the difference, which you know from the running tally, put it in your pocket, and put the rest down in the safe. Perfect, right?"

"I'm not doing it."

"Okay, you don't have to. Just cover for me, okay?"

"What do you mean, cover?"

"I mean like, just, you know, distract Mr. Baum or something."

"How do I distract him?"

"I don't know. Show him your boob?"

"Gross!"

"I know. He *is* gross."

"And a dick!"

"Exactly, Shelli." I put my hand on her shoulder. "That's why we're stealing from him. Because he is a dick."

Can you believe that in the middle of all my devious masterminding, the door swings open and Logan McDonough appears? Shelli nods over and there he is, right at the register, leaning in.

"Um. I'll have a Coke. And fries."

"You don't want a Bunza or anything?" I ask.

We have to say that. It's not like I care.

"Nope."

"Okay, um, that'll be . . . two dollars and seventeen cents."

He doesn't even say anything. He just kind of puts the bills and change on the counter.

"Oh, exact change, thanks."

He's not even looking at me. It's like he's turned inside out or something.

"Can I speak to the manager?"

"Um. What?"

"I'd like to speak to the manager, please."

Oh God, do you think he heard me? I wonder. Do you think he heard my diabolical plan to steal from the Bunza Hut and is going to rat me out?

"Um . . . okay, sure."

Shelli is not a person anymore. She is just two giant eyes standing by the soda machine. Watching.

"Mr. Baum? Uh . . . there's someone here to see you. . . ."

Mr. Baum comes out, taking off his Bunza hat and standing there like a rump roast. Thank God *this* isn't the day we nearly poisoned him to death. At least today, he has the ability to stand. Also, walk.

Logan speaks up. All of a sudden he's like a guy from *Sesame Street*.

"Hello, sir. I'd just like to tell you . . . you have a real top-shelf worker with middle management potential here."

What. Is he. Talking about?

Mr. Baum nods, totally confused.

"Never has a French fry been served up with such love. Such kindness. And I really think you should be proud to have this young lady as a part of the Bunza family. I give her five out of five stars. For customer service. And general friendliness."

Now Logan takes his fries and drink and waltzes out, leaving the front counter of the Lincoln southeast Bunza in silence.

Mr. Baum turns to Shelli and me.

"Friend of yours?"

Shelli and I shake our heads emphatically "No no no no," although I'm not sure why.

"Oh, well, good job then. Nice work."

He goes back to mixing Bunza meat. Shelli and I stand there for two seconds staring at each other, in silence, before we burst out laughing.

"WHAT the?"

"I know!" Shelli can't believe it either.

"Seriously?"

"I KNOW!"

Now we can barely control ourselves. We should no longer be wearing the Bunza uniform. We are no longer representing the store in a responsible manner.

"SOME-body li-ikes yo-ou." Shelli says it in a singsong.

"Shut up."

"And you know what—"

"Don't. Don't even."

"I think you like him back."

"No. I don't."

"Yes, you totally do."

"No, I swear to God I don't."

"Really? Does that mean you don't give him *five out of five stars?*"

Of course I have to throw my towel at Shelli. God, it is such a relief when Becky's not around. Shelli and I are free when she's off doing whatever she's doing. Probably looking at herself in the mirror. But that doesn't matter right now. All that matters is what Logan McDonough just did was kind of rad. And weird. And maybe he might just kinda sorta be a lot more interesting than I, or anyone, thought.

five

If you turned a Labrador into a person you would make Brad Kline. He's happy and gushy and about as interesting and complex as a tree stump. But he's the most popular guy in the school and he's Becky's boyfriend. Of course. As far as I can tell the most interesting things about him are his complete inability to see Becky's true nature and his brother, Jared Kline. Yes, THE Jared Kline.

See, I like a guy who looks like he's just about to rob a bank. And Jared Kline looks like he's been on a Bonnie and Clyde bender for six months straight. Scruffy. Jagged. Mean. Where Brad is a puppy dog, Jared is a wolf. A big, bad wolf that your mother told you about but now you're just gonna have to ignore your mother. He's just out of high school.

And he was never the captain of the football team, or the soccer team, or even track. As far as I can tell he was, and may still be, the captain of the smoking-pot-and-listening-to–Pink Floyd–after-school team.

Anyway, his name is flying all over the place this morning because the rumor is he got Stacy Nolan pregnant. I know. It started in first period, just a whisper, and now, just before lunch, it's a crescendo where it seems like any second the principal is going to announce it over the loudspeaker.

Becky's obsessed. She's practically up before the bell and into the hallway, right next to Stacy Nolan's locker. It's annoying that Shelli and I have to stand here and wait while Becky does whatever dumb thing she's up to, but it's an unwritten rule. We must comply, or die.

I swear to God Stacy sees her and tries to duck away, but it ain't happening. Becky waltzes right up to her, smirking over her books.

"Aren't you gonna invite us?"

Shelli and I stand back, cringe-ready.

Stacy shifts from her right foot to her left. Her face has gone so pale that her little nose freckles are standing out way more than usual. She can barely even make eye contact from underneath her thick brown bangs, because she knows the blow is coming. God, this is painful.

"To what . . . ?"

And now, Becky leans in. *"To your baby shower."*

I notice there is a bit of a crowd around us and everyone is laughing at Becky's little quip. Isn't she just *hilarious*, folks?

Poor traumatized Stacy lets out an involuntary *"eep."* She turns and scurries down the hall like a rat that's been kicked in the guts. Becky looks back at us for approval. But I just can't muster up anything other than a huge pit in my stomach for poor pregnant pariah Stacy Nolan.

The crowd starts to disperse and now Becky's just standing there like she's daring us to challenge her.

"What's the matter with you guys?"

There's nothing for Shelli and me to do but mutter to ourselves. I think we are actually making up new words to mutter. Some of the pep squad girls continue to titter over Becky's little show. We just keep our eyes on our Trapper Keepers and shuffle off to class. After the last bell, we slink away for our long and cruel walk home.

The first three blocks, we don't say anything. But there's no question that the thing we're both not talking about is Becky.

Everyone loves her, yet she is pure unadulterated evil.

The weird thing is . . . It's not like you can point to anything that made her that way. It's not like her dad's a criminal or her mom's a crack addict or she was raised in an orphanage or something. That would actually *explain* her demonic powers. It's just like she was born, she did a few print ads for the Penney's catalog, and abracadabra-BEELZEBUB!

The only possible justification is that, potentially, when she was in the nursery, a dissatisfied ghost of some sort crept into her crib, possessed her baby body, and decided to wreak havoc on the living as revenge for some unanswered injustice. That's really the simplest explanation.

Whatever the case, we are slowly becoming her demon-underlings.

And that is not a job I signed up for.

We're about six blocks from school, the air thick as Jell-O, before it comes up.

I speak first.

"That was SO. LAME."

"I know."

"I mean, seriously."

"I KNOW."

Beat.

"Do you think it's true?"

"What, that she's pregnant?"

"Yeah."

"Kinda."

Beat.

"We have to do something."

"Like what?"

"I dunno, stand up for her or something."

"No way! We can't!"

"Wull, why not?"

"Why not? Are you kidding? Because we've got a good situation here, considering. I mean, you get to be . . . ethnic sorta and I get to make out all over the place and neither one of us has to be tortured about it!"

Beat.

"Well, what if we start a new group of friends or something?"

"Are you crazy? Becky would CRUCIFY us. Not to mention whoever we could get to be friends with us. Which would probably be nobody."

"There's gotta be something we can do."

"Look, if we cross Becky, forget it. She'll turn on us and it'll be, like, vicious. You know it will. It'll be like two seconds before I'm a total prostitute and you're like . . . the n-word."

"The n-word?"

"Yup. The n-word. And she'll, like, add something. Like she'll call you a . . . a vampire n-word."

"A vampire n-word?"

"Yeah. A vampire n-word."

We walk on. It's getting dark. The sun is thinking it's about to set. We've both got chills now. The trees are getting black and spiky. Like they're just about to reach out and strangle us.

I have only one thought.

Jesus. I do not wanna be called a vampire n-word.

six

Our house kind of looks like a Pizza Hut, if you wanna know the truth. We used to have the best house ever, this farmhouse on the outskirts of town, with a barn and everything, but we got kicked off of it so they could build a Walmart. So, now it's Suburbs City and a house where you might as well just drive up and order breadsticks.

Tonight my mom's making pot roast. I get to cut the carrots and leeks and stuff. This is the safest thing for me to do without poisoning everybody. I'm no Betty Crocker. My poor mom has tried with me, but now she knows it's impossible for me to cook without spacing out and burning everything. Plus, who wants to spend all that effort, all those hours and concentration, on something that some ogre is just gonna wolf down in two seconds and burp? The whole thing is just so gross.

I can't help but think about Stacy Nolan. What's she doing right now? Is she in bed, crying? Did she switch schools yet? Is she really pregnant with Jared Kline's baby? More than anything, I just feel bad. We shoulda done something. We shoulda tried to defend her.

"Honey, is something bothering you?"

Peel. Cut. Slice.

"No, not really."

"Are you sure?"

My mom is such a little muffin about everything. Most girls pretty much hate their moms right now, like, you should see Becky. But my mom kind of knows just the right amount of distance. She never squashes me with affection, and she never takes me shopping. And, come to think of it, she never really gives beauty advice, like Shelli's mom. Shelli's mom is big on beauty advice. She'll talk to you so long about Color Me Beautiful, this makeup she wears, it'll make your eyes roll back. But not my mom. She just kinda shuffles us off to school after breakfast—eggs, pancakes, sometimes French toast—comes home at five, and starts with the dinner rotation. But, you know, she checks in kinda. It's like she cares or something.

"Okay, maybe there is one thing."

Peel. Cut. Slice.

"Well . . . do you want to talk about it?"

"Stacy Nolan is pregnant."

"M-hm?"

"And everyone knows it."

"M-hm?"

"And everyone's talking about it."

"M-hm?"

"And Becky did something kinda like really mean."

"M-hm. What did she do?"

"Well, she kinda like . . . went up in front of everyone and asked her if we could come to her baby shower."

"That's not very nice."

"I know."

Peel. Cut. Slice.

"You shoulda seen her face. It was like we punched her."

"We?"

"Well . . . Shelli and I were right behind her."

"Behind Becky?"

"Yeah."

"And you didn't say anything?"

"Nope."

"Hm. Well, how does that make you feel?"

"Horrible. I feel horrible, Mom."

Peel. Cut. Slice.

"Well, maybe there's something you could do to feel better. Could you call—what was her name? Stacy?"

"No way. Becky would freak."

Exhale. My mom is so sick of hearing about Becky. Shelli she likes. She doesn't mind it when Shelli comes over. But she knows Becky is the dark side of the force.

"Well, I'm not going to tell you what to do but . . . I think you should say something to the girl. She's going through a hard time and maybe you could even—"

"That's it!"

"Excuse me?"

"That's it! You have to TELL me to go apologize. If you tell me to, or I'll be grounded, Becky can't say anything because it's your fault."

"My fault?"

"Yeah. If I'm gonna get in trouble if I don't, that can be my excuse."

"Hm."

"Okay, so say it. Tell me I have to go apologize."

"Dear daughter, you have to go apologize."

"Or I'll be grounded."

"Or you'll be grounded."

She's putting the rump roast in the oven now, those funny little grandma-mittens with burn stains all over the place covering her hands. The print is mice on a farm.

Whose idea was that?

"Mom, thanks! I'll be home for dinner, I promise."

The pot roast goes in and I go out. Out into the evening sky, the sun starting to turn the trees into gold dust.

It's about five blocks to Stacy Nolan's house. My plan consists of going up and knocking. I wish Shelli could see me. She would totally die.

seven

Stacy Nolan's house is bricks painted white, with black shutters and a red door. It's a nicer place than our pizza house, that's for sure. Her dad's an eye doctor or something. Normally, I would be jealous. But not now.

I should probably think of a better plan than this. But lo and behold, I'm here on the steps and before I can stop myself my hand goes up to the gleaming brass knocker and—

Knock knock knock.

The door opens quicker than I thought. Like maybe they saw me coming up the step or something. It's her mom. I can tell, when she opens the door, she knows something's wrong with her daughter. Maybe not what. But something. She's hesitant. Protective. Mama bear.

"Yes?"

"Hi, um, I'm . . . I go to school with Stacy and I wanted to talk to her."

"You do?"

"Yeah, I wanted to . . . apologize kinda?"

"I see."

She disappears and then Stacy peeks out from the end of the hall. Boy, she does not look happy to see me. It's like I'm the cops or something.

"Stacy, honey, this girl's here to see you"—now she whispers—"to apologize."

Stacy looks up, puzzled. She steps to the door wary, like, *is this a trap?*

Now she's in front of me.

"Hey, um. Hi." God, this is painful.

"Hi."

"So, um, I feel really bad about what Becky said today. Both of us do. Shelli and me. Like really bad. Especially 'cause"—whisper—"you know."

"It's not true though!"

"What?"

"It's not even true! That's the thing!"

"It's not?"

"No way."

"Are you sure?"

"Uh, yeah. I don't even know Jared Kline. I mean, he's hot and all. But I don't know him. Like, he doesn't even know who I am. Unfortunately."

"I know he's hot, right?"

"Yeah."

We smile. I bet this is the first time she's smiled today. Poor girl. It sucks because all anybody has to do is just say something once, and then everybody just assumes it's true. Like, guilty until proven innocent.

"Well, so you think someone just started it?"

"Yeah, I do."

"Well, do you know who, or like, is somebody mad at you or something?"

"I don't know. I mean, not that I know about."

"Hunh."

Looking at her closer, I can tell she's been crying her eyes off.

"You know what? I can fix it. Like, I'll start in first period."

"You will?"

"Yeah, I know what to do. You'll see."

Her face, which was tiny and turned in on itself, now gets big and glowing. Then there's a big smile on it. She's looking up at me like I'm Mother Teresa or something.

"See you tomorrow," I say. I give her a confident nod, then turn and walk down her steps.

Dang, I think as I hit the sidewalk. *I sure hope I can figure out what to do.*

eight

There's a way to do this and this is how it goes. First, confirm that Becky is out in the morning because of some kind of orthodontist's appointment. Then, walk up the school steps. It's a crisp morning where summer is giving up to fall. Gaze at the foliage contentedly until Jenny Schnittgrund comes up panting.

"Did you hear?"

"Hear what?"

Jenny Schnittgrund has been trying real hard for the past two years to move up a couple of notches in the social hierarchy. Little does she know it's never gonna happen because Becky smells her blood and desperation, and that right there is the reason she's doomed. Despite the new clothes, trips to the mall, and season pass to Tans-R-Us, Jenny Schnittgrund will never be anything other than a minion at best.

"Stacy Nolan is pregnant!"

You stop, you consider. Wow. Jenny really is the color of an Oompa-Loompa.

"And Jared Kline is the dad!"

Here goes, folks. Let's hope this works.

"You didn't hear? That's this other Stacy girl, from out in Palmyra." And this is the part where I lean in, confidential. "And it's not even Jared Kline's. I know 'cause I know the guy. He's a total dog."

Jenny Schnittgrund leans back. It's like I told her aliens are landing after sixth period. Her feet are five minutes behind her brain, which is already racing to tell everyone and anyone the news. A scoop!

She looks at me, nods her head, grateful for the confidence. I can tell that maybe she even thinks she's popular now.

We swoop into the school and the rumor is coming along beside us. Jenny and I part ways and I get to go straight, in a line, to my locker, but the rumor goes this way and that way, from Jenny's mouth to that girl's ear, to that group of guys by the bike rack, in through the door, to those two girls at their lockers, past the principal's office, past the teachers' lounge, through the rocker guys, and into the ears of Pep Squad

Girl, who heads me off on my way to homeroom.

She practically bowls me over, books in hand.

"Did you hear?"

"Hear what?"

"It's not Stacy Nolan who's pregnant. It's this other Stacy. This girl from out past Palmyra." She leans in, an expert. "I know, 'cause I know the guy, and he's a real dog."

"Really?"

"Oh, yeah. Total. Dog."

Wow. My exact words. Verbatim.

Now that is what I call success.

I nod and duck into my classroom.

You should see Stacy Nolan. She's sitting there all by herself. It's weird 'cause she's perfectly still but you can practically feel her trembling. God, she's in a panic.

Now for the finishing touch.

It's here that I'd like to mention that this is the trickiest maneuver of the routine. Like, if I nail this, the Russian judges will award extra points. If I don't, it could be a complete disaster. I could end up ostracized alongside Stacy for, well, life maybe.

Instead of taking my desk, in the front, 'cause I'm kind of a straight A student thanks to my vampire dad, I sit right smack dab next to Stacy. She looks up like I have just landed from Mars.

I whip out a *Seventeen* magazine from my backpack and put it in front of us. The way she looks at me, it's like I'm James Bond or something.

"This October issue is so gay. All it is is back-to-school and Halloween parties. Again."

Stacy Nolan takes her cue. Yes, she is supposed to look now. Yes, she is supposed to act engrossed. We pretend to look through the magazine together.

"Eww. That guy's gross."

Beat.

"How'd ya like to kiss that guy?!"

Beat.

"YUCK! Look at this one! What a douche!"

Beat.

"Oo, I like that. Is that Guess?"

Beat.

"Cool shoes. I like those leg warmers with them."

Stacy is just nodding away by my side, but that's not what's really happening. What's really happening is the room is starting to get crowded, people are starting to trickle in, one by one, and see us. See me. Third Most Popular Girl in School. Together. With Stacy Nolan. The one who, just yesterday, was pregnant.

But today? Well, today, she is flipping through magazines with number three over here.

They start to swarm.

First, it's the pep squad girls. Then, the hair-spray girls. Then, the heshers. Then, the brainiacs. And now for the coup de grâce . . . Charlie Russell. Yes, if Charlie Russell bites we are home free.

Charlie is the de facto mayor around here. Everyone knows him. Everyone is his friend. He's nice enough, but if you asked someone why he's such a big man on campus, I doubt they could tell you. Maybe it's because he plays tennis, wears rugby shirts, and lives in a ginormous mansion on Sheridan Boulevard.

Charlie sits down right beside me. Praise Jesus!

"Morning, ladies. To what do I owe the pleasure?"

"This dumb mag, look how stupid."

If you woulda told Stacy Nolan that by first period, before the first bell, she would be surrounded by the pep squad girls, the hair-spray girls, the heshers, the brainiacs, Charlie Russell, and yours truly . . . looking through a *Seventeen* magazine amongst a chorus of oohs and aahs, she woulda sent you to a funny farm. But here she is, Stacy Nolan, the erstwhile Pregnant Stacy Nolan, the center of attention again, but now, in a good way. Beyond redeemed. Perhaps even more popular. Having avoided a scandal and all.

The bell rings and everybody takes their seats. I go back to my suck-up seat in the front row. Before Mrs. Kanter gets to her speech on the history of the cotton gin, and southern productivity in general, Stacy Nolan looks at me across the room. The awe on her face? You would think I was the tooth fairy.

I smile and wink and she just mouths it.

"Thank you."

Even though I am made of spider stew, there is a part of me that doesn't mind feeling like this. Like maybe, maybe it's possible I did something kinda sorta good.

And I would relish this moment. I would. If I didn't know that I was gonna pay for it, dearly, when Becky finishes at the orthodontist and hears what happened.

nine

Just like I thought, Shelli and I are leaving school, beginning our zillion-mile walk home, when here comes Becky.

"What the fuck?!"

Oh God. This is gonna be bad. Shelli just looks at the sidewalk. She knows what's coming.

"What's going on?" I ask.

"You know what's going on. Immigrant."

People are starting to look and this has the potential to ruin me. I dunno. Maybe I shoulda never stuck my neck out. Dumb conscience. Thanks a lot.

"No, I don't."

"Really? Two words. Stacy. Nolan. Ring a bell?"

"Oh, yeah, my mom is SO. ANNOYING."

Becky stops. "Wait. What? What does your mom have to do with it?"

"She totally made me go over there last night and APOL-OGIZE. It was SO. LAME."

And now I do a three-second eye roll.

"She did?"

"Yeah. It was like. Excruciating."

"What was her house like?"

"Kinda stupid. I dunno, it was like, her dad has those fake ducks everywhere."

"Fake ducks?"

"Yeah, like mallards. I think that's what they're called."

"Did it smell?"

"Totally. It totally smelled like soup. Even the lawn kinda."

"What a loser. I can't believe you were talking to her."

"I know! But, like, I had to. My dumb mom was gonna ground me."

"Really?"

"Yeah, for like a month."

"No way."

"Way."

Now we all sigh, a collective sigh against the injustice of moms.

"It was SO queer."

"Sounds like it."

Thank God Brad Kline comes barreling up. He puts his arm around Becky, who would look smug that she's bagged the most popular guy in the school, if she didn't look annoyed he was wrinkling her dress.

"Dude. Party at my house. Friday night. Be there."

And now he nods at me.

"'Specially you. Chip likes you. You know that?"

Chip Rider is the second potato on the popular guy front. He's blond and blue-eyed and looks like a Ken doll had a baby with a Cabbage Patch Kid.

"So, you coming?"

"I guess so." This guy Brad, seriously, has the IQ of a toaster oven.

He's got twenty dolt friends calling him over, so, praise the Lord and pass the cornflakes, he and Becky steer off into the abyss of jocks. Becky says something that has the jocks and all of their would-be girlfriends/hangers-on in stitches.

Shelli and I duck out to our long days' journey into the sidewalk. We are halfway down the block before we each let out a huge sigh of relief.

"Dude. That was close."

ten

What our folks are thinking, making us do this annoying long walk home every day, is beyond me. First of all, it's starting to get cold. Late September is about to grab ahold of all that sun and fun, shake it up, and turn it into fall harvest fest, fright night, Homecoming, turkey day, and then the big Christmas explosion. But what that means right now is: cold and getting colder.

It's only like forty degrees today, the sun starting to set and Shelli and I forgot our coats. By "forgot" I mean we rolled our eyes when our moms asked where they were.

Shelli's mom is a real freak. Like, she's a total Christian and is always talking about what would Jesus do, and the real meaning of Christmas, and how to hate gay people. If she only knew that before her very eyes she was raising her own personal Mary Magdalene, her eyes would probably roll into the back of her head and she'd start speaking in tongues.

Here's another thing: She calls me Mexican. Yes, ladies and gentlemen, according to Shelli's mother I am her Mexican friend. Never mind that Shelli has told her a million times I'm half *Romanian*, and that I never see my dad anyway. No, sir. I'm still a señorita from south of the border. I guess an immigrant is an immigrant to her but it gets not so amusing because Shelli actually had to beg to be friends with me after her mom found out. I'm not kidding. Shelli had to actually beg her weirdo mother for days to let her be friends with a half-breed like me. Her mom had literally said, and I quote, "I don't want no daughter of mine hanging around with a beaner." End quote. Can you believe that horse manure?

Shelli was loyal, though. She went on a hunger strike till her mom had to give in. Still, I don't exactly like sticking around when she comes home from work.

Before then, though, Shelli and I have a whole tradition. When we get to her house, since it's halfway between school and my house, we plunk down, eat cookies, drink hot chocolate, watch MTV, read magazines, and gossip about guys she likes. We should probably lay off the cookies but don't forget it's getting cold out, so that makes it impossible, really.

Cookies are not meant to be today, though. Once Becky went off with Brad Kline and his festival of jocks, Shelli and I thought we were in the clear. We got about five blocks from school and guess who came riding up on his moped?

Logan. McDonough.

Shelli looks at me like it's the Hells Angels.

"*What do we do what do we do?*"

"Act casual."

He pulls up on the corner in front of us, so it's not like we can ignore him. He takes off his helmet, squints at the visor.

"You wanna ride?"

Shelli and I look at each other. Which one of us?

"You. Anika." Then he says it again, to himself kinda. "Anika."

Shelli looks at me, whispers, "Um. Freak?"

"I'm gonna," I whisper back.

"No, you can't!" Now Shelli seems actually scared.

"Why?"

"You know why."

"Do you think I'll burn in hell?"

"No. I think Becky will torture you, slowly, and you know it."

"Well, don't tell her."

"She'll find out."

"No, she won't."

"She'll totally find out."

"It's just a ride. It'll be . . . our little secret."

And now I'm off to get on the back of Logan McDonough's moped. Can you believe? He looks like he can't either. He stares at me like he never thought in a million years this would work, but also like his chest just got inflated.

I look back at Shelli.

She's in some kind of catatonic state. I wave. Even though she wants to be mad, I know she can't be. There's a part of her, no matter how small, that kind of loves this. Drama!

Logan hands me his helmet and guns it off the corner. If I told you how many times my mom has lectured me not to get on the back of a motorcycle, which I'm assuming correlates directly to a moped, you would think I'm the world's worst daughter for not giving it a second thought. But then you'd be forgetting that (1) It's cold, (2) It's almost two miles home, and (3) Logan seems to have suddenly, overnight, turned into that guy in that old black-and-white movie, down by the docks, the one with the funny mouth, saying, "I coulda been a contender! I coulda been somebody!" Or that other one, where he just yells "Stella!" all the time.

eleven

Have you ever flown through the air with the greatest of ease? Have you ever had the trees and the wind and the houses and all the noise in the world you've ever heard just whiz by and off and up above you and next thing you know it's like you could whoosh up into the evening sun and maybe past that, too? Up, up, up into the bright orange sky and off this stupid, everyone-talking-at-the-same-time earth? Well, that's what it's like on the ride home with Logan. We are flying through and past and over and around, zooming zooming past everything and everyone that does and doesn't matter. My mom was right to tell me not to get on one of these. I am hooked.

Poor Mom. She tried.

By the time we make it to my house, the sun is dipping down into the trees and everything's turning orange orange orange. Logan stops about two blocks past my house, so my mom doesn't ground me until college. If my stupid sisters were home they'd torture me for the rest of my life for this, and call me a slut. Mostly because, you know, goose/gander and all that.

I get off the back of Logan's moped and expect him to ride off into the sunset but he gets off, too.

"Walk you to your door?"

"What?! NO!"

"Why not?"

"Are you kidding? My sisters will ambush you."

"You have sisters?"

"Uch. Yes. Two of 'em. And they're super-annoying."

"I have two kid brothers. But they're kind of cute, actually."

"Oh, I have two brothers. They're older. They're not so bad, either. They leave me alone at least."

"Your sisters are probably just jealous. You know that, right?"

"I don't know. I just wish they would ignore me or something."

The sun's coming in rays through the trees and I'm terrified someone will see me. Maybe even Stacy Nolan. Now that would be a reversal of fortune.

"You know what I think?"

He's got a sly smile now. I should hurry back but something is making my feet disregard this command from my head.

"I think you're hard to ignore."

"*Tsh.* What is that supposed to mean?"

"I think you're beautiful."

"Shut up."

He smiles and I am just about to obey that command from my head to get out of Dodge, but then something happens. Something that's supposed to not happen and is not the reason I stepped on that moped. No way.

"I'm gonna kiss you now and you're gonna like it."

And he does. And I do.

!

Right there two blocks from the house, Logan McDonough is officially my first kiss (yes, I know, late bloomer) and I don't really know how this is supposed to go even though I have seen a lot of movies that could act as reference. But none of that matters now because, essentially, I'm having an out-of-body experience where I can't believe, can't believe this is happening but I can't stop don't want to stop no way nohow.

Before I know it, or know which way is up or what year it

is, anyway, Logan leans back and smiles at me like he knew it all along and he's glad I know it now, too.

He dips his helmet like it's a cowboy hat.

"Happy trails."

And now that helmet is back on his head and now the moped is up and running and he's halfway down the street and I am left to stand there and wonder what the hell just happened. And I may be just fifteen and don't know very much, like maybe it's kind of like I don't know anything, but I know this—

I am in serious trouble.

twelve

Pedaling fast fast fast, this is the moment. This is the sky turning from black to purple to pink and now the sun coming up and I am still not fast enough. Not fast enough to change it.

Pedaling fast fast fast, this is the sun coming up through the trees and there's nobody, nobody on the streets, nobody on the sidewalks, nobody but me and the light coming off the pavement. Nobody for miles around, the entire universe holding its breath in silence, but in my head a thousand voices, in my head, a chorus, an orchestra, a stadium.

Pedaling fast fast fast, this is the moment and there has to be a way to change it, there has to be a way to stop the earth from turning, there has to be a way.

thirteen

"I just want you to know, I hired a black girl. Don't be scared."

It's late afternoon at the Bunza Hut and Mr. Baum drops this news like he's telling us the Rapture has begun. Shelli and I stand in silence at the soda machine.

"Why would we be scared?"

Nothing.

"What's she gonna do, eat us?"

Mr. Baum, and every other adult I know, seems to actually think this stuff makes some kind of difference. Even smart people. It's weird. And you can never get them to talk any sense about it because it's like it's important to them, having something to hold themselves over. Some*one* to hold themselves over.

Usually it just comes across as something ridiculous Shelli and I laugh at later over hot chocolate. Except when it's not funny. Except, for instance, up in Omaha, there was this kid from halfway across the globe that hardly spoke any English and got transferred here from some refugee program where I guess no one was really thinking. He was in school at Omaha Northeast for two days before he had the shit kicked out of him and every bone in his body practically broken. When he recovered, which thank the Lord above he did, they transferred him out of this white-bread state and back east somewhere. You could never believe the pictures they showed of him on the news. That purple face and those eyes. God, that was the worst. Looking into those eyes. They might as well have just said, "Why me?" on the top of each lid. It made your skin crawl.

That's why I gotta keep a low profile about my half-breed roots, which, thank God for Becky Vilhauer, I can. That is what she is good for. Protecting me from getting spit on in the hall on a daily basis. Or worse. A purple face and a "why me" written across my eye sockets.

But now the kid who *does* get spit on at school, on a daily basis, comes into the Bunza with his mom, his dad, and his baby sister.

Joel Soren. He's nice enough and just looking at him it's

hard to tell why he, particularly, has been singled out for such daily ridicule.

It started with Becky, of course. The whole thing was so stupid. She asked him for a piece of Hubba Bubba, watermelon flavor. He only had one left and he was giving it to some pep squad girl. Like, he was literally handing it to her when Becky asked for it.

So Joel Soren ignored her.

And didn't give her the gum.

So Joel Soren had to pay.

He pays with his books getting tossed out of his hand. He pays with his ankles getting tripped down the hall. He pays with his locker getting "Nerd-face" or "Super-gay" or "Fag" tagged on it every other week. Not that he is gay. And not that it matters. They just write it. The jocks. Becky doesn't even bother. The whole thing has taken on a life of its own and he's just everybody's punching bag for no reason other than a five-cent piece of Hubba Bubba.

The lesson is not lost on me.

Shelli nudges me as Joel and his family come to the register. I swear to God she's rung up like three customers in the eight months we've been working here. To be honest, she may be kind of scared of the register. Or maybe she can't add. She *is* a Christian. I don't think they believe in math.

"Three number threes, with fries, and a kid's meal, for

the little one here."

I look over the counter at Joel Soren's little kid sister. She's a three-year-old towhead with big blue eyes and a giant pink pacifier.

"What a little cutie! What's her name?"

"Violet."

"Aw, what a pretty name."

Joel Soren isn't even looking at me. He's hiding behind his parents, pretending to look at the glass door, which is about as interesting as a cement block. I feel bad for him. Does he think I'm gonna spit on him, too? Does he think I'm involved in this constant humiliation?

Am I?

"Well, thanks. Oh, and three Cokes, please."

"Yes, sir. That'll be nine dollars and fifty cents."

Shelli stands back at the sundae machine as the Sorens scuttle off to their seats, a family unit.

"Don't you feel bad for him?" I ask her.

"Yeah, kinda," she whispers.

"I mean, doesn't it seem, like, unfair?"

Mr. Baum pokes his head out. "Order up!"

Joel's dad comes back to the counter to collect the food. I mean, it's not like this is the Sizzler or anything. You gotta bus your own food at the Bunza Hut.

Shelli checks her hair in the sundae machine.

I stare at the back of Joel's head. "I'm gonna go over there."

"Why?"

"I dunno. I just feel bad is all. And lookit him. He's mortified!"

"Yeah, but, what are you gonna say?"

"I dunno."

"You're queer."

"Shut up."

Shelli play-swats me.

"Stop making passes at me at work. Lesbo."

"Hnnn. Lez be friends . . ."

Shelli is seriously like a five-year-old. But I'd rather be stuck next to her any day of the week than Becky Vilhauer.

I walk over to the family unit, eating their family dinner at the Bunza Hut on a Thursday night, and Joel Soren looks like he wants to crawl under the table and turn into a pill bug.

"Hi there, is everything to your liking today?"

"Yes, thank you." It's the dad talking. The man of the house.

I'm trying to make eye contact with Joel. Smile or something.

"How about some refills?"

"Oh, no thanks."

"What about some ketchup, do you want some ketchup?"

"Um, no. We're fine, thanks."

"Mustard?"

"I think we're fine on the condiments, thank you."

"Okay, well. Enjoy your meal and thank you for coming to Bunza Hut!"

Yeah, maybe that didn't work so well. I think I just annoyed the dad.

Look, all I was trying to do was make Joel Soren feel like a human being for once. I mean, can you imagine going to school every day and getting shoved around, your books knocked down?

God. Becky doesn't even control it anymore. That's how powerful she is. She just started the snowball. And now it's an avalanche. With poor Joel Soren buried underneath.

fourteen

My parents are under the distinct impression that it is impossible to sneak out of my room. Wrong! I can understand why they think this. If it were anybody else, and not a criminal mastermind like myself living in this fortress, it would, indeed, be impossible. Here's the thing: I specifically chose this room because it appeared to be impossible. That was my second move. My first move was to figure out that it was, actually, possible.

Anyway, tonight's gonna be easy because all anyone cares about is this weird thing that happened down in Oklahoma. Some guy found out his wife was screwing her boss at the Kmart. That's not much, I know. But then the guy thought the best thing to do was to go to the Kmart, shoot the boss, shoot the wife, and even shoot all the people around who didn't have anything to do with it in the first place.

All in all it was six people dead, including the guy. My mom won't stop freaking out about it. She doesn't have her head on straight, though, because if she put two and two together she'd figure out that number one: That guy was an Okie. Number two: That's two states away. And number three: There isn't even a Kmart in Lincoln; the closest one is in Omaha. So, basically, if she'd just face facts for a few seconds she'd breathe easier knowing that things like that just don't happen here.

I kept trying to get it through her head all night but she's stuck on it. I mean, she was watching the news like it was the *Hindenburg* or something.

Which, in the end, is good for me. And my diabolical plan for sneaking out.

This is how it works. The bedroom is on the second floor, and there are two windows, each a long rectangle that is only about a foot and a half high. Now, add to this that the windows fold out in the middle . . . and you are talking about a space of about nine inches to get through. Also, there's nothing to latch on to. Even if you manage to somehow magically squeeze through that tiny slot . . . what are you supposed to do, just fly away?

Except. And there is always an except. There happens to

be an oak tree with a branch that comes about two feet away from the window.

So, here's how you do it: You tell your parents you want to go to bed early so you can get enough sleep for that big test tomorrow, which is imaginary, of course. They smile at you and pat themselves on the back for thinking you are such a good person and that they have done such a good job raising you.

Then, you wait. At some point, they'll go to their room, at the other end of the hall. The TV light may be on, but that doesn't mean anything. That thing could be on all night, and into the next century, believe me.

Once their door has stayed shut for about fifteen minutes, you put on whatever crazy thing they wouldn't let you out of the house in if you were walking out the front door. Except for your shoes. You have to drop your shoes to the ground. You're gonna need your feet. Trust me.

So you crank open the window, drop your shoes to the ground, then breathe a big sigh in and out. You have to make yourself as skinny as possible to get through that sliver.

Now, put your feet up on the bed and reach out of the window, so that you're basically in a Superman position, parallel to the ground.

Now. Reach out the window, stretch as far as you can, and grab the tree branch. Don't be scared. Just grab it. Yes, I know it's weird to be in a Superman position stretched like Gumby out the window grabbing a tree branch but it works, trust me. Okay, now make sure you have a good grip on the tree branch and pull pull pull until you are practically out the window completely.

Alright, now this is the hard part. This is "the move." What you have to do now is you have to, basically, use the momentum of swinging out the window to get your feet to the nearest lower branch to hook onto it, like a monkey. If you screw this up you'll fall. And possibly die. That's okay though because at least then you won't have to take your SATs.

Once you have executed that last monkey move you are home free. All you have to do is crawl down the tree and voilà! There you go past your annoying sisters, who are probably flirting on the phone with guys who just want to get into their pants, past your brothers' room, where Robby is probably watching sports on his mini TV and Henry's got his face in his chemistry textbook because if he doesn't get into Harvard, he'll die.

Who cares though 'cause outside it's freedom!

Okay, I'll admit it: I'm meeting Logan tonight. Don't tell. Shelli has some idea there is something going on because those moped rides home from school are getting more and more frequent and, to be honest, more and more super-fantastic. Now that we're into fall—and once the sun goes down you start to freeze your boobs off—these moped rides are kinda sorta where it's at.

We haven't been kissing all the time so get your mind out of the gutter. It's more like . . . he'll swoop by, pick me up, and next thing you know we'll be flying over the hill and through the tract housing and the world is our oyster but we don't have to talk about it. Like, we don't have to talk about anything. And sometimes we'll kiss good-bye without even saying anything. And then he'll pass me all sorts of funny little notes, furtively in the hall between bells, but we don't say anything there either. In fact, there's a whole lot of not-saying-anything going on here. It's kind of like we're spies.

The thing is, Logan is a lot smarter than all those dumb no-neck guys on the football team. Especially Chip Rider, the one everybody keeps saying I'll die if I don't like him back. What a rube! He thinks Chekhov is a *Star Trek* character. I mean, like, if you said to him, "Actually, the Chekov you are thinking of, the one from *Star Trek*? Well, that guy was probably named after the more important Chekhov, who is a super-famous playwright and basically like the Shakespeare of Russia." If you said that, he would just stare at you with a blank face and then his teeth would fall out.

Meanwhile Logan has probably written like five plays secretly that are obviously brilliant but no one will know because they're just sitting there in his Trapper Keeper.

Since all you can think about is kissing, here's a point of interest: Logan is a really good kisser. Not that I've kissed a lot of guys. And by "a lot of guys," I mean "anybody." But I have seen a lot of movies and I think I get the general idea. Also, and I may be wrong about this, I think there's a direct correlation between how much you like someone and how much you like kissing them.

For instance, if Chip Rider was the number one kisser in the universe, world champion five times over, and he kissed me . . . I bet I wouldn't like it as much as I like kissing Logan. See? That's my theory. I haven't put it to the test, though. And I can't ask Shelli because, well, first of all, she bones anything that moves and, second of all, then she'll figure out that Logan is more than just a moped ride-share. Becky is out of the question, for obvious reasons. And, of course, I can't ask my mean sisters because they will just harass me endlessly, tease me, tackle me, pin me to the ground, and then spit on me. I know. They totally suck.

Henry won't know either because the only girl he's ever made out with is Princess Leia in his dreams and, possibly, his *Sports Illustrated* swimsuit issue. Now, Robby, on the other hand, probably has kissed a few girls but I'm pretty sure there is absolutely no useful information he could give to me on the subject because he's a boy and I'm a girl. He'll probably just say something stupid like, "Yeah, it gives you boner."

Anyway, it's pretty cold out. There hasn't been any snow yet but tonight the grass is freezing over and you can see your breath. None of this has stopped me from wearing a completely weather-inappropriate outfit and yes, that's a miniskirt. But I'm used to the cold and I'm wearing tights anyway. Besides, I've got thermal socks under my boots so by the time I meet Logan I'll only be half-frozen to death.

He says he has a surprise for me and I know that's the kind of thing serial killers say before they haul you off to a hole in their basement somewhere and start dressing you up like their mom before they strangle you. But, considering that we've been on over thirty after-school moped rides together and not once has he asked me if he could cut off my scalp and use it for a bonnet, I think I'm in the clear.

Besides, tonight is one of those nights when I'd really like to stick it to the man. And by the man I mean Count Chocula. See, my dad's pissed because I'm getting a B in PE. But I'll tell you why. Every time we have to do something big like run a six-hundred-yard dash, or climb the ropes, or leap tall buildings in a single bound, every time, like clockwork, it's the day I've got my period. And not even a small day like the fourth day or fifth day, but like the first or second day, when it's like you might as well be in the emergency room.

I mean, who wants to run the six-hundred-yard dash when you're bleeding like a stuck pig and it feels like everybody's punching you in the back?

And the ropes? Forget it. Can you even imagine that?! There was this girl in eighth grade, Carla Lott, who got her period the first time in white shorts and it leaked and everybody knew. Everybody. From then on it was just Carla Lott! Period Spot! Carla Lott, Blood Spot! For *years*.

And I'm gonna tell you something. Every girl, every girl you've ever met, dreads, DREADS, that ever happening to her. Every one. Even Becky. It's no fair. Guys don't have anything like that. I mean, if there was any justice in the world you wouldn't even have to go to school during your period. You'd just stay home for five days and eat chocolate and cry.

Anyway, what's gonna happen is Count Chocula is gonna call any day now, super-early, like 6:00 a.m., and explain to me that As are better than Bs and that if I want to get out of this one-horse town and go to a good college on the East Coast, I have to be a straight A student, no exceptions, no excuses. And, if I don't, then obviously, I will end up a full-fledged loser, living barefoot and pregnant and married to some guy named Cletus, in the middle of nowhere, with all my hopes and dreams dashed.

Like my mom.

He won't say that part, but that's what he means. Believe me.

So tonight it's time to say fuck it.

I'm about two blocks from Holmes Lake when I see Logan parked on his moped behind a weeping willow. He doesn't see me yet so I get to take a good look at him and decide if I still like him, despite the fact that if anybody finds out about our torrid affair, I will be ousted, blacklisted, and shunned.

I'm trying so hard not to like him. It would be so much easier not to like him.

But, unfortunately, he's not making it any easier on me because he's just sitting there with his dirt-brown hair looking like some beautiful-but-grimy-but-tough-but-heart-broken-but-earnest-but-guarded fallen angel or something. I mean, he might as well have his own theme music. Something dark. With lots of keyboards. And some violins.

Ugh.

Why can't he just be a dork?

I walk toward him and his eyes catch me. "You ready for a night of spontaneous super-specialness?"

That's the other thing that's hard to stop liking about Logan. He doesn't say anything the way anybody else says it, or maybe even think anything the way anyone else thinks it. Like, if this were Chip Rider, he'd be like, "Hey, yer hot!"

But there is Logan, standing now, in all his misunderstood, complicated glory with cool turns of phrase and cooler thoughts behind them.

I really can't take it.

I hop on the back of Logan's moped and all of a sudden we are flying past Holmes Lake and down, south south south, past the outskirts of town and into this weird new mini-world of new and practically new and half-built houses. There's a turnoff with a sign in cursive, like something off a bottle of wine, that says, "Hollow Valley." We take it and inside the development the houses are three times the size of the ones on my block. They're bigger, even, than the house down on Sheridan where the mayor used to live.

These places are, like, new but are trying really hard to look old with lots of turrets and arched windows and ironwork and stuff. But it's also like you could push them down, like they're a movie set or something.

They're all halfway built or almost done or just the foundation, but there, at the end of a street called Glenmanor Way, there's a three-story monstrosity ready for its close-up.

And that's where we're headed.

Logan pulls up in the driveway, doesn't even try to hide or anything, cuts the engine, and gets off.

"Home sweet home."

"You're kidding, right?"

"Kinda."

He walks up the stone path toward the giant front double doors and starts reaching into his pockets, making a squiggly mouth.

"It's my dad's new thing. His latest investment. This is the demo."

"Demo?"

He finally plucks the key out of his pocket and now we are in a massive faux-marble entry hall, fully decorated with fake plants and everything.

"It's like a model house," he explains. "So when they go to sell the other houses, people can walk through and ooh and aah until they sign the check and pop the champagne."

I have to admit, even though it's 100 percent super-fakey in here, it is nice. Like so nice my mom would probably freak out and start bumping into the furniture or something. There's even fake grapes in a fruit bowl and a fake bottle of champagne on ice.

Logan sees me looking at the demo champagne and reads my mind.

"There's beer in the fridge 'cause my dad likes to loosen up the clients if he gets that vibe. Especially the guys. You know, *man talk*."

In the middle of the house is a giant room that the upstairs looks down on from a railing, and a fireplace with fake plants on each side.

"Here's the best part."

He reaches next to the fireplace and presto, there's a fire in the fireplace automatically.

"Wow. That was easy."

"Yeah, I think that's one of the big selling points."

He hands me a beer, a green German beer with a white label.

Logan explains, "My dad likes to keep it classy."

I grab the beer and we clink bottles.

"Is your dad, uh, classy?"

At this point Logan spits up his beer all over the rug. It's hard not to laugh.

"Wow. An actual spit take."

Logan wipes his chin. "My dad is so not classy. He's like a used-car salesman in an expensive suit."

"Aw, that's not nice."

"He's not nice."

Silence.

"He like goes on all these so-called fishing trips and bones everything that moves and then comes back with some stupid mallard decoration and expects us all to believe it."

"Really?"

"Oh, yeah."

"That sucks."

"I know. And my mom totally buys it. So do my kid brothers. It's so lame."

"Well, how do you know?"

"If I tell you, you're gonna be like so grossed out."

"Okay, well, now you have to tell me."

We're sitting on the demo couch now, some faux-suede L shape sunken in front of the fireplace.

"Okay, so one day he told me he wanted to go fishing *with me*. Like you know, father-and-son stuff, and so we went up to Madison together, in Wisconsin, on this big *bonding trip*."

"And?"

"So then, the first day we get on the boat he's like, 'There's someone I want you to meet' and next thing you know he's got this little chippie behind him getting in the boat. In heels. Heels, on a boat! It was, like, mortifying."

I make a note-to-self about boat-appropriate footwear.

"Are you serious?" I ask.

"Yeah."

"What, like, he didn't think you would care that he was cheating?"

"Guess not."

"He didn't think you would care *about your mom?*"

"Nope. It was like 'we're all men here' or something."

"That's so gross."

"I told you."

I am silent. Seriously dumbfounded. "What a dick!"

"I know."

"Did you tell your mom?"

Logan lets out a sigh and drinks his beer a second.

"No. I'm lame. I can't. I don't know what to say. It'll like ruin her, you know?"

"Really?"

"Yeah, she's like really fragile, and kinda in love with him, and scared of him in a way."

There's a pause and now it all makes sense, the brand-new moped, the new wardrobe, the new everything, to Logan from his dad.

It's all a bribe.

Something Logan said sits funny with me. "Why do you think she's scared of him?"

"I don't know." He is silent for a moment.

"He's just kinda weird, you know, like he can't sit still or something. Like we can't go out to dinner without him looking around the room like a thousand times. And all he does is brag about stuff. The things he buys my mom. The places for dinner. Like we should all be so grateful. And when we're not like all falling over ourselves to kiss his ass he gets like . . . I dunno."

Logan and I sit there staring into the fire for a minute. I

guess we both have shitty dads. Maybe everybody does. That would be something. Maybe the single moms everybody gets so apoplectic about are onto something.

I think about my mom, having that ogre snoring in the bed beside her, and I shudder. Seriously.

But at least he doesn't sleep around all over the place. The only thing the ogre cheats on my mom with are his French fries.

"You know, Anika. If this is too weird to be here, I get it. I mean, it's kinda like, a fake house or something. Well, it's exactly a fake house, actually. Some people might find it a little . . . freaky?"

"No. No, it's not freaky. I'm happy we're here."

"You are?"

"Yeah. I mean I snuck out, didn't I?"

We both sip our beers and stare at the fire.

Silence.

"You're like the prettiest girl I've ever seen in my life."

He blurts that out. I can't help but gasp. He covers his face with his hands. "Oh my God, I can't believe I just said that. I'm so lame. Please don't leave."

I recover. "Tsh. What? Why would I leave?" I shake my half-empty bottle at him. "I mean, I think this is kinda like the best bar in town. It's certainly the cheapest."

He smiles. "Right."

"Besides, it's . . . Nobody's ever said anything like that to me before."

"No way."

I shrug.

"I don't believe you."

"Well, it's true. What, do you think people just go around telling people they're pretty all the time?"

"Not people. *You.* I think people must say that to you every day."

"Um. They don't. They say it to Becky . . ."

"She's a cunt."

"Whoa!"

"She is."

It's hard not to smile at this. Such sacrilege.

"Come on, you don't think that your dear friend Becky is an A-number-one velociraptor in disguise? I mean, she's a total sociopath."

"Um. I think I plead the Fifth."

"She is. You know she is."

We're both smiling now.

"Come on, admit it."

"Never."

There's something in the air between us. Like a magic trick.

"Well . . . I suppose . . . I should take you home now."

"What?"

"I should take you home. I don't want you to get in trouble."

"Aren't you gonna try to molest me or something?"

"What?! No! You're crazy, you know that, right?"

"I just thought it'd be sort of funny."

"Funny?!"

"Okay, okay. I wasn't gonna let you anyway."

"Well, isn't that like the definition of molestation?"

"Just forget I said it, freak."

"You're the freak."

"No, I'm not."

"Yeah, you are. You're the sexually deranged freak."

Now the demo couch pillow gets tossed in his face. And, of course, he tosses it back.

I don't want to get on his moped and go home. I don't want to walk out these giant demo doors. I don't want to do anything that makes any single tiny minuscule atom in this room change. I just want *this this this.*

fifteen

"Anika, Shelli, I'd like you to meet Tiffany." And he whispers, "The *black* girl."

Shelli and I stand there next to the sundae machine at the Bunza Hut, while poor Tiffany, skinny and incredibly shy, follows Mr. Baum in next to the front counter.

"Hi."

"Hi."

Mr. Baum smiles a ridiculous fake smile. He seriously looks deranged.

"You totally pull off that uniform better than me." I don't know what else to say, so I just say it. It's true, though. A yellow polo and Kelly-green shorts is not an easy look to pull off. Let's face it. I look like a can of 7UP. But this girl? She's kind of rocking it.

"Oh . . . thanks."

She is rocking it in the most painfully shy way possible.

"Well, Anika, I'm counting on you to show her the ropes!"

"Yes, Mr. Baum."

Of course he doesn't even look at Shelli. I guess she won't be showing anyone any ropes around here anytime soon.

"Anika, do you mind if I talk to you, in private?"

"Um . . . okay."

Mr. Baum hustles me into the back office—it's really more like a closet with Post-its everywhere. Violation central.

"Anika, I know you probably are not happy with this situation. For obvious reasons."

"Really? Like what?"

"You know."

"You know what?"

"Because . . ."

"Because what?"

"Because she's a . . . negro."

"A *negro*?"

"Yes, Anika. And I need you there to make sure she understands . . . the concepts."

"The concepts?"

"Yes."

"What, like, if you buy a combo special it's fifty cents cheaper?"

"Exactly."

"Wow. Um—"

"Listen, I need someone up there who's smart. You're a straight A student—"

"That's an accident. I'm only a straight A student because if I'm not my dad won't love me."

"Is that true, Anika?"

"Pretty much."

"Well, I'd like to talk to him sometime—"

"You'd have to call Romania, or Princeton. He goes back and forth . . . It's kinda hard to figure out where he is, actually."

Silence.

"Why don't you have Shelli teach her?"

"C'mon. Shelli's a bubblehead."

"So, Shelli's a bubblehead and Tiffany's a negro. Geez. You know, I'm Romanian. What weird thing do you think about me?"

"It's possible you might be a vampire."

"Mr. Baum. I don't mind helping. But, seriously, I think you should maybe give this girl a chance."

"I am giving her a chance. I hired her, didn't I?"

Poor guy.

He has no idea I'm stealing his profits.

And poisoning him.

But, in my defense, I think this conversation kind of proves he deserves it.

Thank God it's a slow night and we get out of there early. On the car ride home with Mom, I can't help but think about Tiffany and how stupid Mr. Baum is. It doesn't seem fair he just gets to think all this horrible stuff right off the bat and meanwhile she's just like this skinny little thing that probably needs a job real bad. I know they say that's the way the cookie crumbles and all. But you can't help but wonder why there's any cookie-crumbling going on in the first place.

We pull up at the 76 gas station.

"Mom, how come we don't go to church?"

"Oh, honey, that's just a bunch of nutjobs."

"Wull, Shelli's mom goes all the time."

"Look, if you wanna go, go, but when they start thumping that Bible, talking about right from wrong, who's naughty and who's nice, who's gonna get to heaven and who's gonna burn in hell, you might want to start to look for the exits."

Beat.

"If you want to talk to God, all you have to do is put your hands together and pray."

Beat.

"Seeing as he's everywhere and all." Then, to herself more than me, "Bunch of hypocrites. Sitting around judging all the time."

Beat.

"Never judge a man till you walk a mile in his shoes."

Beat.

"That way, you're a mile away and you've got his shoes."

She winks. My mom's kind of queer but I can't help but smile.

"I better fill up the tank. You stay put."

She jumps out and slams the car door.

sixteen

It's one of those dumb days where nothing's really wrong but nothing's really right either and the sky can't even choose to be white or gray. It's a Monday, of course, which also makes everything stupid. And I don't know why, but I just have this feeling of dread, or depression, or some other word that starts with a *D* that makes you want to just crawl back in bed and pull your pillow over your head.

There are some positives. For instance, I have managed to avoid Becky all morning. I got an A on my biology test. And, according to the cafeteria menu, there will be cupcakes.

But other than that, the whole thing is just drab and pointless.

Also, Logan doesn't pass by at his usual time for us to

pretend we totally don't know each other and aren't secret spies who are maybe madly in love or something.

Kind of annoying.

Right now I'm in the only cool room in the school, which is where we have art class. They built this annex way after they built the school with someone who actually seemed to care about what things looked like . . . natural light, the way the ceiling slopes, and, generally, creating an environment where a bunch of artistic teenagers wouldn't want to throw themselves off the nearest bridge.

To their credit, it worked. You do get the feeling when you walk in the room that something vaguely interesting could possibly happen here.

But that also might be because our teacher is stoned.

Did you know there's something called marijuana? Yeah, you smoke it and all of a sudden you grow long hair, eat Cheetos, and listen to Pink Floyd till your mother knocks on the door to tell you to clean your room, or at least wash your hair, or possibly consider doing something with your life.

There's no question in my mind that Stoner Art Teacher had other plans.

I know I should probably know his name by now but I can't remember his name and that is probably because he can't remember his name.

I bet he thought when he grew up he'd be riding a motorcycle across the country like Che Guevara or Jack Kerouac or something but so far his stoner habit has only led him to teach a bunch of sulky teenagers how to paint trees.

That's what the sixties were for, I think. To turn everybody into losers. Also, to make sure everybody wore socks with sandals.

Whenever old people tell you "you had to be there" and the "sixties were groovy" or whatever, just listen to the words of my mother: "Oh, honey, most of those people were just idiots. Sheep, following along. Remember that. Whenever you see everybody clamoring in one direction, do yourself a favor, go the other."

But right now we're in class, learning about legendary Pop Art icon Andy Warhol. I am creating a masterpiece involving a series of identical ice-cream cones in a perfect pattern, with different ice-cream colors. Stoner Art Teacher is impressed so it is clear I will be running off to New York after graduation in a beret.

All this hot art action is brought to a screeching halt by the fact that the fire alarm goes off and next thing you know we are all scuttling out the door.

Outside on the lawn we're the only class huddled together because our little architectural outpost is set off from the rest of the school. It's freezing but everybody seems elated by the novelty of being outside. OUTSIDE! IN THE MIDDLE OF THE DAY! Never mind that we were just outside, like, two hours ago.

After about fifteen minutes of elation leading to amusement leading to boredom, we are dutifully hustled back in and there is nothing really to report.

Except.

Remember my ice-cream Pop Art I was telling you about?

Well, that's been replaced.

Well, it hasn't been replaced, actually, just set aside.

For a greater work.

I know. You're dying to know what it is.

You and everybody else in the class. Including Stoner Art Teacher, who I do believe is freshly stoned.

This is what is currently gracing my easel: Imagine, if you will, a painting made of white, oil, glass, mirror shards, more glass, more white, even some newspaper and magazine scraps painted over white. All of this stuff is on the canvas. And so, when you first look at it, it kind of just looks like a bunch of white stuff that catches the light and sparkles and is sorta kinda dazzling.

But then, look closer, now you see what the picture actually makes. The shards and the glass and the painted newspaper and the oil all come together to make an image, a very faint image, of a girl. Of a girl with jagged cheekbones and a square boy-jaw and purple raccoon eyes with white-blonde hair and gray-blue eyes who looks kinda sorta like . . .

"It's you!"

It comes out from the hesher section of the mob.

"Hey, Anika! That's you!"

"It totally is!"

"Did you make that?"

And now everybody's looking at me. And now I'm just shaking my head. I mean, what am I supposed to say? (1) I'm not that talented, and (2) Yeah, I just made that when we were all standing outside together freezing our faces off—with my mind.

Now comes Stoner Art Teacher.

"Hm. This is actually kind of interesting . . . Mixed Media. Monochromatic. Yet, there's something almost frenetic about it, kind of like a Jean Dubuffet . . ."

Wow. I guess Stoner Art Teacher actually read some books along the way between bong hits.

And now he turns to me.

"Well, Anika, looks like you've got yourself a secret admirer . . . A very talented one, at that."

I say a silent prayer in which I thank God Becky's not here. If she were, there would be swift and immediate punishment. Both for being the subject of this tribute and for the tribute being, I'm certain, made of trash in Becky's eyes.

But it isn't trash.

And when I think of the diabolical way in which its author ensured its delivery, I feel that magic in the air. Electric. Like there is a live wire nearby.

No one knows the artist's name.

But I know the artist's name.

I smile.

Logan.

seventeen

I know you probably think Shelli bones all those guys because she's in love with them, but here's the funny thing, I don't think that's it. I think she just does it to spend time with them. Like, they all go out and all the guys are wondering the whole time, which one of them gets to bone Shelli. So, it's like she gets all this crazy attention while they hope they'll be the one. She bones down with one of the guys, then just leaves him, like doesn't say good-bye or kiss him or anything. She just jets out of there like a house on fire and never talks to the guy again. Ever. Doesn't call. Doesn't write. Doesn't stalk.

What's funny is that this makes them like her more. Like she just has this superhot sexy sex with them, ditches them, and then all of a sudden *they're* in love with *her.*

I gotta hand it to her, it's kind of genius.

I know I couldn't do it. Especially 'cause I'm totally petrified of contracting some grody disease. You never know with these guys. Some of them look like they are like straight out of juvie. I don't know how Shelli keeps 'em straight, but they do all keep trying to fondle her—all the time.

Shelli's weird racist Christian mom made her work at the Bunza Hut to keep her out of trouble. The irony of this isn't lost on me, considering that I'm rapidly turning her into a first-class saboteur.

But tonight she can't even go out to Brad Kline's birthday party because her mom has suddenly decided she has to stay home and study the Bible or something.

One of these days her mom is gonna get taken away to the funny farm, I swear to God. Her mom makes her burn her hair after she gets a haircut, so no one tries to cast a spell on her. I'm serious. That's the level of loony tunes we are talking here.

So, tonight it's just Becky and me, which may sound like torture except for two important factors:

Number one, Becky is completely different when she's in party mode. It's like she's just copying all those girls from teen movies and her goal is to be the life of the party, the belle of the ball, the shiniest of the shiny, the super-happiest!!

So she's making Jell-O shots and smiling it up and acting like she's just the coolest raddest hottest girl in the US of A.

I know. It's surprising. But even Darth Vader has a few red buttons.

As much as I normally wish Becky would get swallowed up into the nearest sinkhole, the fact is, when she's in this mode, you kinda can't help but like her. She's charming and funny and she'll get the party started and bring you in under her wing and make you sing out loud to the cheesiest songs and laugh like nobody's business.

This solidifies her reputation as the Number One, Super-Fantastic Becky Vilhauer that everyone just HAS to be around—just HAS to make their friend.

I couldn't hold court like that. I'd totally punt it. But Becky does have something. She just only takes it out on special occasions. And this, my friend, is a very special occasion.

That's the second thing.

The party is at Brad Kline's house. This means a Jared Kline sighting is imminent.

Yes, THE Jared Kline.

I swear every girl here is just waiting to see if they will see a glimpse of The Great One, and maybe, just maybe, get to talk to him. Or even blow him. That's like a goal.

I know. It's hard to believe the guy is that kind of a rock

star. But he is. It's epic.

Even I, with my disdain of all mankind, cannot resist a peek at Jared Kline. I'm not standing in line to defile myself with him like all these other girls . . . but . . . I don't mind looking at him. It's kind of like seeing Jesus in a tortilla or something.

The Klines live in this huge Tudor house on Sheridan Boulevard that looks kind of like they should be selling chocolate in Bavaria. And, of course, Becky is here because Brad Kline is her boyfriend. There is one serious damper in their relationship at present, which is that Becky is in the back room, right now, having sex with Brad's brother.

Like I said, no one can resist Jared Kline.

Not even Becky.

My job right now is to make sure no one, particularly Brad Kline, goes anywhere near the back room. It's not an easy job, but somebody has to do it and considering that Shelli is probably at home reciting the New Testament with Mama Crazy-Pants, this duty has fallen on yours truly.

To say that there is a lot of puking at this party is an understatement. Lucky for me, the two upstairs bathrooms are near the front of the stairwell, so I just have to stand here and sway like I'm drunk but not really in a hurry to go anywhere while Becky gets herself inducted into the hall of fame for Kline brother fucking. I hope there is a condom involved. That could be one tricky DNA test if something went wrong. . . .

Mostly I just wish Logan would magically appear in the window, possibly in the form of a bat, and then we could fly away to some dark and spooky mountain where he would have to make out with me just to keep me from crying.

But that doesn't seem to be happening.

What is happening, right this second, is much worse. Brad Kline is stumbling up the stairs drunkenly looking for his girlfriend, who is ten feet away, boning his brother.

What to do, what to do?

Brad Kline is captain of the football team, so tripping him on the stairs might actually result in the varsity football team never making it to State. Such an event would be the closest thing to the nuclear holocaust in these parts, owing particularly to everyone's vicariously living lame parents, and would probably end up with me being sent to a high-security prison where I would be constantly violated by girls with names like Spike.

So, I can't trip him.

Also, it's his birthday.

Now he is lumbering straight toward me and is about to crash right into that room and, ladies and gentlemen, that is not going to be a pretty sight. Or maybe it would be a porny sight. But whatever sight it is it's probably going to lead to a Cain-and-Abel fight to the death, using knives, rapiers, or perhaps just fisticuffs. They were both on the wrestling team at one point so there is a good chance it will look a little like Homo City, whatever happens.

Before thinking it out in any way, I grab Brad Kline by the jersey, throw him up against the wall, and shove my tongue down his throat like I am a sex-deprived nymphomaniac just back from an island of frogs. Brad is utterly confused but not so confused that he doesn't kiss me back. It is here that I would like to state that Brad Kline is a terrible kisser. It really is like his tongue is a lizard that is trying desperately to eat everything inside my mouth and then slither down my throat. Gross!

It occurs to me during this lizard-slithery kiss that this could backfire mightily and Becky could actually get mad at me for protecting her slutty self in the back room with Brad's brother.

So now what?

It's here that I decide that the best thing to do is pass out. Which I do. And how. Yes, folks, it's official. I am now lying on the ground as if someone hit me over the head with a hammer.

Chaos. Anarchy.

Frogs are falling from the sky.

Suddenly the big drama at the party is that Anika, Becky's

second-best friend, is blacked out cold and oh my God, what if she doesn't wake up, we heard she's a vampire anyway and now maybe she is part of the undead!

Now everyone is saying we should call an ambulance, no, we should not call an ambulance, yes, we have to call an ambulance, no, we can't, we can, we can't.

If I opened my eyes, which I want to do so badly it's eating me alive, I would see a circle of heads above me, pondering, debating, squinting. All I want is for that damn back door to open and Becky to get the hell out here so my grand charade can come to an end.

But, instead what happens is Jared Kline.

Yes, THE Jared Kline.

Next thing I know, Jared Kline is picking me up, like he just married me, and carrying me down the stairs to the library. The crowd parts like the Red Sea at the sight of The Great One carrying this broken-winged bird down the stairs and into the dark wooden den, where he is obviously going to save my life by issuing CPR and turning me into a fairy princess.

No one is playing opera, but they might as well be.

Everyone tries to clamber into the room with us but Jared sets me down on his dad's giant desk, turns around, and slams the door. As I open one eyelid to peek at who is outside looking in, I see something that fills me with dread.

Dread!

No, it's not an ambulance, or the cops, or even a horde of drooling body snatchers. It's Becky Vilhauer, standing there, looking at me like I am dead meat.

Which, let's face it, I probably am.

eighteen

"Hey, hey . . . are you okay?"

Now's the part where I have to pretend I am waking up from my blacked-out slumber.

My sister Lizzie used to put us in plays all the time, mostly musicals, so it's not like I don't have any experience flexing my thespian muscles. We were so good, in fact, that my mom even put us on the talent circuit. We used to have this whole routine we'd do to "Ain't She Sweet," which would really rake 'em in. I was the ringer. My sisters would do a toe-step, sing their part. Then my brothers would do a soft-shoe, sing the chorus . . . and then I would come on with a giant lollipop and a huge hat and next thing you know we'd be getting that state fair trophy. True story. You could practically hear the sighs of defeat from the other contestants when I stepped on the stage. The only time we ever got second place was when we were up against a chicken that played tic-tac-toe. That day, the chicken was the ringer.

"Anika? It's Anika, right? Becky's friend? Wake up, Anika!"

Waking up from my fake blackout, trying to look dizzy, and looking straight into the face of The Great One . . . well, that, my friends, was not hard. He's standing right above me looking down at me like I am the tiniest, sweetest, and cutest of bunny rabbits.

"Are you okay now? Here's some water."

The room is made of dark cherrywood and there's a kind of green glass lamp on the desk, green felt on the dark wood mahogany desk. I never thought to wonder what the Kline brothers' dad did for a living . . . but whatever it is, it's not too shabby. This house, the room—the pictures on the wall, oil paintings with ships stuck out in huge choppy waves in the middle of the ocean, the ladder you can move around to get books off the shelves—this is like something you'd see in *Trading Places*, not Lincoln, Nebraska. Lincoln's the kind of place where, if you're rich, you have two cars. Not a library room with a ladder and nautical paintings.

I drink from the glass in silence, looking up at Jared Kline, trying to figure out what to say that doesn't make me sound like a complete idiot. "So, you just had sex with your brother's girlfriend" probably won't cut it. He's not saying much either. Just kind of staring at the rug. Some Persian-looking thing, also expensive, flopped in the middle of the parquet floor.

This is a room to impress people. And it's working.

I venture a small thanks.

I hand him back the glass of water and he just sits there. I'm waiting for him to swing open the doors and go back to his mad, passionate affair with Becky Vilhauer.

It's strange though, it's like he just wants to sit there in a trance, staring at the rug, and making me feel stupid.

"You know, they teach your dad's book in Modern World History. Gustav Dragomir? That's your dad, right?"

I blink. "Yeah, that's him alright."

"Smart guy. You know he's really famous, right?"

I shrug. "Whatever."

"How come you don't live with him?"

"Well, he lives in Romania half the time, so . . ."

"You live with your mom?"

"Yeah."

Um, discussing Count Chocula? Is the last thing I thought I'd be doing at this party. Things I thought I *would* be doing: Jell-O shots with Becky, jumping off the roof, riding a bicycle into the swimming pool. (By the way, I've actually done that last one. Just for the record.) But definitely not this.

"You must be smart, too, then, huh?"

Jared Kline is known for a lot of things. Getting stoned. Making out. Breaking hearts. Being a stone-cold fox. But smartness? Well, if he's anything like his brother, that's not part of the skill set.

"What kind of question is that?" I ask him. "There's no way to answer that without sounding like an idiot."

He smiles at that, looks at me.

"I'd offer you some weed, but I think you're kind of on the road to recovery here."

"I know. I'm sort of embarrassed." I move to hop down from the desk. "I guess we should get back to the party. . . ."

He glances toward the door and squints.

"I'm not really in a hurry. You can, if you want."

Well, the one thing I'm not gonna do is leave gorgeous Jared Kline in this gorgeous room for no reason. I may hate all of mankind but there are certain things you just don't do. Even if you are a misanthrope. Walking out right now is one of them.

This is surely one of the most awkward moments in the history of Brad Kline's dad's library. Both of us are just sitting there, not knowing what to say. But here's the weird thing, it seems almost like Jared Kline is . . . nervous. Could it be? The Great One gets nervous?

"So, are you and Becky best friends or what?"

"I dunno. Kinda."

"She's not a very nice person, you know."

This is a weird thing to be coming out of the mouth of someone who was just having sex with Becky.

"I plead the Fifth."

"You shouldn't hang around with her."

Now I am becoming vaguely annoyed. Who is this person to tell me what to do? This is the first time we've even spoken, for crying out loud. Just because he carried me all Scarlett O'Hara down the stairs, doesn't give him the right to boss me around.

I scowl my scowliest scowl. "Oh, yeah, who *should* I hang around with?"

And now he looks right at me for the first time, a weird sort of look I've never seen from anyone, except in movies.

He leans in and says, in barely a whisper—

"Me."

nineteen

I never got to grow up in rich-people rooms. Rooms in suburban houses with paneled walls and maybe a super-sweet
TV, sure. But a room like this, with an ornate globe and
nautical paintings and green felt, for some reason? No. This
is the kind of room you get born into.

I'm not crying to myself here, or pretending I've been
raised in a shack or something. I haven't. My mom made
sure of that by marrying the ogre. That was her sacrifice.
And I know it. I know it even if she doesn't want to admit it.
She made a trade. And she did it for us.

I can't help but wonder if it was worth it. And I can't
help but want to do something to someday make her proud.
Although stealing Mr. Baum's face off at the Bunza Hut is

probably not a good start.

But, here, now, at Brad Kline's party, stuck in this rich-people room with THE Jared Kline . . . it's like I might as well be on that episode of *The Brady Bunch* where Davy Jones comes to visit Marcia and she practically floats down the stairs.

But I also know that anything Jared Kline says is a big fat lie because he's a scam artist of legendary proportions. A wolf in a Led Zeppelin T-shirt. Everyone says so. And right now he's just sitting there, kicking his Vans up on the desk and smiling at me like he knows something super-fantastic but can't say it.

"Look, I know you are a total scam artist, so I don't know what you think you're doing here to me but I just want you to know it's not gonna work."

He shuffles his Vans.

"Oh yeah?"

"Uh, yeah. I'm pretty sure you can't be taken very seriously."

"Really?"

"Sorry, but I'm not gonna lie to you, I know everybody thinks you're like God's gift to the universe but that doesn't mean that I think that or that I'm just gonna take my pants off or something because you saved me, like I'm some broken-winged bird. You probably just saved me because you didn't want to be liable or something."

"Liable?"

"Yeah. Liable. Like you didn't want to get sued or something. I know that stuff happens all the time so . . ."

"It does?"

"Yeah."

"Like, give me an example."

"Well, okay, well, I can't think of anything right this instant but I know that people do that. I mean, my mom is always saying don't have people over because if somebody gets drunk and gets into a crash you're liable to get sued."

"So, your example is your mom talking about a hypothetical?"

"Yeah. It's my mom. My example comes from my mom."

"Do you like your mom?"

"What? What kind of a question is that? Of course I like my mom, crazy."

"Okay, well, I just want to make sure."

"Why, do you not like your mom?"

"Yeah, I love my mom. She's really into trying to help other people. Especially, like, kids with cancer and poor kids and stuff. I think it's pretty cool, actually."

I guess this is his way of trying to show me he has a "heart" and that I should like him. But I am not taking the bait.

"PS," I tell him, "I just want you to know that I know you

just had sex with my friend Becky, so if you're going for some sort of trifecta, or second-fecta, or whatever, it's not gonna be happening."

"Second-fecta?"

"Yeah. You know. Like sloppy seconds or whatever."

"I didn't do anything with Becky."

"Yeah, right."

"I didn't."

"Come on."

"Seriously? She like threw herself at me and I had to kinda tell her that wasn't cool. Seeing as she's my kid brother's girlfriend and all."

"I don't believe you."

He shrugs. "She's not your friend anyway."

"What's that supposed to mean?"

"She's nobody's friend. She's like a dragon . . . wrapped in a cute girl."

"Huh. Well, how do you know I'm not the same thing?"

"I never said you were a cute girl."

I imagine Jared can see the steam coming out of my ears. "Thanks. Well, I'll just be leaving now—"

"I think you're a cool girl."

Okay, so maybe this stops me.

"I think you're a cool girl who happens to be kind of hot, actually."

"Okay, listen, I don't know what dumb lines you are used to giving girls so they fall all over you but I just want you to know that I wasn't born yesterday so I am gonna go now and leave you to whatever dumb idiot girl is gonna buy that line."

And now I walk out the door. But just before I get there, I hear him.

"Bye-bye, cool girl."

twenty

Of course the first person I see out of the door is Becky.

"You are so dead."

The party is emptying out now and she's just about to turn and walk out the front door, so now I have to hurry to catch up to her.

"What? Becky . . . I'm telling you. I was trying to cover for you."

"Listen, immigrant. I don't know what's gotten into you lately but you are getting a little too big for your britches, if you ask me."

"Becky . . . I was covering for you. Hello? Brad was coming right up the stairs . . . it was like a total disaster. *Titanic* heading for the iceberg."

"So, that's why you had to run off with Jared?"

"I didn't run off with him! He carried me! Do you know that whole thing was for YOUR benefit so you wouldn't get busted? Hell-o. I was being a good friend to you. I, like, fainted to cover for you."

Becky stops at the front door. If she turns on me my life is gonna be a living hell, I just know it.

"What did he say? You were in there a long time."

"Nothing, I mean. Really . . . all he did was talk about you."

Beat.

"He did?"

"Yeah. It was like kind of crazy. He's, like, obsessed."

And now she drags me out the front door and under a giant oak tree that is thoroughly decorated in toilet paper. This lawn is a floral bed of beer cans.

"Okay, so I want you to tell me *exactly* what he said."

"Um. Well, basically, he was just like saying how beautiful you were and how he wishes you weren't going out with his kid brother so he could be your boyfriend. And maybe take you to prom even."

"What?! No."

"Seriously. He thinks you're like a supermodel or something."

"Well, I *did* do that catalog shoot a month ago," she says

more to herself than me. "Do you think I should break up with Brad?"

"What?"

Now the whole party seems to be tumbling out onto the front lawn.

"You know, so like I can go out with Jared?"

"Um. I don't think it works like that . . ."

"What do you mean? You just said he liked me!"

"He does! He totally does. It's just . . . He can't go out with you, even if you do break up with Brad. It's like, too mean. You can't go out with your brother's ex-girlfriend. It's like incest or something."

Now the whole football team, including Brad, seems to be sprawling out of the front doors. Chip Rider is puking in the trash can on the curb. Gross.

"Listen, immigrant. I'm not mad at you anymore. I guess I was just annoyed. You know, 'cause he like saved you or whatever. But you're right. Of course he doesn't like you. I mean, no offense, but you are kind of like a half-breed. I mean . . . not to be mean or anything."

"Yeah, no. I mean. That would be crazy."

"And that was really nice of you to cover for me."

"Thanks. Well, you know, what are friends for . . ."

"Hug?"

"Yeah, okay."

And now I am hugging Darth Vader herself while Chip, in the background, thinks he's done puking but isn't done puking, so now he's basically walking around while puking down the front of his sweater.

"You're a good friend, Anika."

It is a wonder I don't puke myself.

twenty-one

It's not lost on me that the only two guys in the universe who seem to somehow, maybe, like me are both completely off-limits for entirely different reasons. What a bizarre world, isn't it? Logan is off-limits because he's a social pariah that could completely ruin me if anyone knew about our moped rides and late-night sneak-outs. Jared Kline is the biggest stone-cold fox in the city, possibly even the state, and if Becky knew the things he was saying in the hoity-toity library, she would hand me to the wolves covered in butter.

Of course, I can't tell Shelli about any of this. I just know she'd slip up. She forgets things, or can't keep them straight. For instance:

Shelli keeps messing up how much money we're stealing.

I don't know what it is—I mean, all she has to do is subtract the amount from CHARGE but yet it's like every time she gets loose change or she gets a ten or a twenty it's like she can't wrap her head around the numbers. I mean, I don't want to call her stupid, because she's not, but this certainly doesn't seem to be her forte. The problem is we can't steal with Tiffany. It's got to be just Shelli and me. But I have a sneaking suspicion Tiffany would actually be better than Shelli with the numbers.

On the other hand, everyone would be looking at Tiffany in the first place because this town is just a bunch of suburban hillbillies in khakis who think, *actually think*, that because Tiffany is black she's genetically predisposed to steal everything in sight. I mean, it's ludicrous.

Shelli's not even here today, 'cause it's Sunday and her nutjob Bible thumper of a mom won't let her work on the Lord's Day or whatever, so it's just left to the sinners Tiffany and me to work on this holy day and burn in hell together.

I am not going to teach Tiffany how to steal. No way. She seems like a really good girl and the last thing I want to do is help anyone in this small-minded town reaffirm their small-minded ideas about skin color and thievery.

But it's tempting.

There was a rush about an hour ago but now the place is like a ghost town. Mr. Baum is downstairs, doing inventory, so it's just Tiffany and me making conversation. Badly.

"Your mom seems really sweet."

Tiffany has seen my mom come in and wait for me before driving me home. My mom has definitely made an extra effort to be nice to Tiffany in order to not be mistaken for a racist. Although, deep down, honestly, I think she kind of is. No offense, Mom, but you're just supposed to be normal. Not nicer. Not meaner. Just normal.

"Yeah. She's a good mom. A lot better than my dad, that's for sure."

"At least you have a dad."

Ugh. I didn't realize Tiffany was just in this thing with her mom and no one else. That might explain why half the time no one comes to get her and my mom and I end up dropping her off. It's kind of a total bummer because her apartment complex on Highway 80 is exactly in the opposite direction of our house so it adds like thirty minutes to the drive home, which is a lot after a day of shelling out Bunzas and French fries to family after family of endless beige people.

I'd be annoyed except you can't help but feel guilty when you see where Tiffany lives. It ain't no country club, that's for sure. There's always a couple of trucks parked out front and one or two beaters that look like they're on their last legs. On those days when her mom doesn't show up, she just kind of runs inside and neither my mom or I ever really know what to say.

I mean, what are you supposed to say? I'm sorry your life sucks so much? I'm sorry your mom never remembers to pick you up? I'm sorry there seems to be no dad involved in this situation?

I have not once got a look at her mom, you know. She always just kind of sits outside in the car and honks the horn. It's a burgundy Pontiac, not a bad-looking car, actually. But I think it's weird how she never comes in or anything. I bet she's pretty, though. Tiffany has really kind of delicate features, like a Kewpie doll. Not to mention her skin is like a dark mahogany with a lightbulb somewhere behind it. I wonder what it's like for her growing up in that crappy apartment complex with no dad and no hurry to get one.

There's about a thousand different questions I want to ask Tiffany but every single one of them seems like the dumbest ever.

For instance: We get a free meal per shift here at the Bunza Hut. Now, Shelli and I never take it because we have had everything on the menu eight thousand times and if I have to eat another Bunza meal in a Bunza I will commit hari-kari. But I have noticed Tiffany eat the free Bunza meal, every time, methodically, like clockwork, including the strawberry shake. She also will eat anything in sight when no one is looking and she weighs about three pounds. This makes me think she's either not getting any food at home, except maybe Frito-Lays and Twinkies, or that she's got the metabolism of a coke addict on crack. Not sure.

In any case, you can't help but wonder if there's something to be done about it. I mean, what if she really doesn't have anything to eat at home? If her mom's consistency at ride-giving has any correlation to her meal-giving, she's in big trouble.

"Hey, you wanna come over Friday night for dinner?"

I say it before I even know I'm gonna say it. Such a stupid idea. What if she thinks I'm feeling sorry for her?

"Sure."

"We can pick you up and everything."

"Yeah, okay. Sounds nice."

And there it is, folks. I have officially invited the only black person in Lincoln, Nebraska, to have dinner with the ogre, my mom, Henry the brooding, Robby the happy, my two slutty sisters, and me this Friday night. I wonder if my mom will make it buffet-style or if she will get out the good china and act like she's Carol Brady.

twenty-two

My dad always calls at like 7:00 a.m., because half the time he's in Romania and the timing over there is something like eight thousand hours ahead, so it's night for him and way too early for me. Top this off with it's always a lecture and you have an all-day-ruiner right there.

"Vhat is dis I hear about a B in physical education?"

"I dunno it's just—"

"Dat is a ri-di-cu-lous class, but nevertheless, it vill count on your transcripts."

"Well, it's just—"

"Listen to me. I do not intend to raise a daughter who ends up barefoot and pregnant living in Nebraska of all places. Besides dat, you vould be mi-ser-able if dat vere your fate."

"I know it's—"

"The reason to get good grades is so dat you vill go to an elite East Coast college, vhere you vill increase your social cap-i-tal by networking vith people whose parents are not construction vorkers."

"I know—"

"Do you vant to end up like your mother, vith a one hundred sixty-two IQ and nothink to show for it? One hundred sixty-two, can you believe it? And look at vhere she is. Is dat vhat you vant?"

"No, Dad."

"Okay, so here is vhat you must do. You find dat een-significant physical education teacher after class. You ask him for advice. People like to feel important. Dis vill make him feel important."

"Okay."

"Den you follow his advice to the letter, every detail of his advice, apply yourself. And den, at the end vhen you have improved, you appear grateful and thank him for his vords of visdom. He vill give you an A. Trust me. Because you vill have made him feel like his seventeen-thousand-dollar-a-year job actually matters. You understand me?"

"Yes."

"Good. Now, put your brother on the phone."

Walking off back into my room I can now hear my

brother pleading for his life. . . .

"Yes, Dad. I got a ninety-eight percent. But I did the extra credit so that makes it a ninety-nine percent. . . . No, he doesn't give a hundred percent to anyone. I am the top of the class. Yes. Ninety-nine percent is the top grade."

I wonder if my father knows how terrified we are of these 7:00 a.m. phone calls from Romania. I mean, in a way, you have to wonder why my mother even puts us on the phone. I wish she'd just relay the message so we wouldn't have to start the day getting freaked out and shivering into our cornflakes. It's like two hours before my heart stops pounding every time.

By the time I get to fourth period, aka gym class, I've almost freed myself from the shackles of this fear and loathing. But . . . Mr. Dushane walks in.

Yes, that's his name, can you believe it? Dush-bag, Dush-face, and my personal favorite, Dush-nozzle. He's been called them all. Behind his back.

He's in great shape, for an old guy, but the funny thing is, he always wears red short dolphin shorts, like really short. You can practically see his you-know-what sticking out of the front of his dumb slutty shorts. What a freak. You definitely get the feeling this guy thinks he's like God's gift to mankind. And womankind. I'm serious. He acts like he just happens to be some Greek god in short shorts set down temporarily to teach us teenage nuisances the importance of the fifty-yard dash. The problem, and the reason I'm getting a B, is: I don't buy it.

But now, according to my vampire father, I have to pretend to buy it. Hook, line, and sinker. How embarrassing.

"I gotta go talk to Mr. Dush-nozzle."

Shelli takes this class with me. Thank God. At least we can sit in the back giggling during Mr. Short-Shorts's monologues about team spirit or whatever the hell he's talking about.

"What? Why?"

"My dad says I have to."

"The ogre or the vampire?"

"The vampire."

"Oh."

Even Shelli knows that's serious.

"Do you think I should do it now?"

"I dunno. His shorts look pretty short today. What if his wiener sticks out and tries to bite you?"

"Gross! Do you think he has a girlfriend?"

"Yeah, and her name is Rosy Palm."

"Okay, here goes."

The last thing I want to do is talk to this guy, but what are you gonna do? If I don't I'll end up barefoot and pregnant and living in a trailer park with a guy named Cletus.

His office has glass around it, stuck right behind the gym. He's doing something with laminated charts and looking vaguely confused.

"Um. Mr. Dushane?"

He doesn't hear me.

"Mr. Dushane? Can I talk to you for a minute?"

"What? Oh, hi. Yes, what can I do for you . . ." He can't remember my name.

"Anika. My name's Anika."

"Right! Right. I knew that. So . . . what can I do for you, Anika?"

"Well, I wanted to talk to you about my quarter report. I got a B."

"Yes?"

"Well, I'm just wondering what advice you could give me, seeing that you're considered like one of the most inspiring teachers and all . . . I'm just wondering, like, what advice you can give me to get better, and, you know, get an A."

"It's not about As and Bs."

"Mr. Dushane, I've never gotten a B before in my life. I'm not allowed, okay?"

"I see."

"And I just want to ask you what I can do to improve myself, here in PE, and I am really just looking for some advice from someone who really seems to have it all figured out."

All figured out? Who says that? What am I turning into over here?

"Okay. Okay, Anika. You have to apply yourself. You have to think, when it seems hopeless, when you're getting tired in the six-hundred-yard dash, you have to give it not one hundred percent . . . you have to give it one hundred and ten percent. See what I mean?"

What an idiot.

I could get that kind of advice from a Nike commercial.

"Yes. Yes, Mr. Dushane, I do. I really want to thank you for that. It really means a lot to me."

He nods, making a reassuring but stern face. A guyface. A jockface, also used by politicians, I've noticed. It says, "This is how it's done, and we can do it!"

Guys are so full of shit.

Okay, back to Shelli.

"What'd he say?"

"He said his wiener wants to meet you."

twenty-three

Shelli's mom picked her up today because she's bringing her straight to Spring Youth. Spring Youth, can you believe it? If you don't know what it is, picture this: Twenty or so kids go over to the leader's house and eat cookies, drink punch, and sing songs. The song lyrics are projected, written out in pen so you can sing along. The leader, or her husband, plays guitar. It's all fun and everyone is having a big old time. Then, the leader, or a guest speaker, gets up and talks about Jesus Christ our Lord and Savior. At the end of each session you are invited, if you so choose, to get up and say, "My name is so-and-so and Jesus Christ is my Lord and Savior."

Now, how do I know this? Because I have attended one

of these Jesus parties and I know firsthand that it is actually extremely enjoyable until Nerdlinger, our particular Spring Youth leader, gets up there and starts talking about Jesus. They should just stick to the songs and the punch.

Anyway, today is Shelli's day to try to be a stand-up Christian but I am pretty sure they don't give out awards for how many guys you've blown by the jungle gym.

The funny thing is, Spring Youth does a better yearly ski trip than the school so I have actually spent one entire week with these people, skiing in Steamboat Springs, Colorado, and listening to the lessons of Jesus Christ our Lord and Savior, from Nerdlinger and other similar yet varied nerd-underlings from across the Midwest. One thing for sure about these guys, they all definitely look like they have nothing better to do.

Basically, if you were casting a film, and you needed to fill the role of a quiet loner, who possibly goes out one day and decides to shoot everybody at the Taco Bell, it would be this guy. And his minions. Thank God they found Jesus, otherwise we'd all be in trouble.

I do have to say, by the end of that week of skiing, and listening to the nerd-minions talk about Jesus, and singing folk songs under that giant wooden hall in the middle of the resort . . . I'm kind of surprised I didn't stand up and find Jesus. I'm sure he was around there somewhere.

But now it's Shelli's turn to be indoctrinated, so this particular afternoon I get to walk four blocks on my own till Logan zips over on his moped and saves me from the brisk October air. And when I say brisk, I mean freezing.

But when Logan pulls up to the curb, he doesn't look happy. He kind of just stares at me with this hangdog look.

"What?"

"Nothing."

"Um, obviously, there's something wrong, so . . ."

"It's just. I dunno. I heard you're with Jared Kline now. Is that the deal?"

"What? No. Are you kidding?"

"It's just, everybody was saying you like left that party with him."

"Oh my God. That is like a zillion percent not true. Here, can I just . . ."

"Look, it's no big deal—"

"But it's not even true! Jared Kline is like a total scam artist. Everybody knows that. Do you think I'm gonna fall for that?"

"I dunno."

"Do you?"

"Well, do you want to?"

"Do I want to fall for Jared Kline and then have him dump me and be a laughingstock? Uh . . . no."

"Yeah, but what if he like really liked you? Would you like him?"

"Logan. What are you talking about? I'm like sneaking out to see *you* and stuff. Doesn't that mean anything?"

"I dunno, maybe you just need a ride home."

"*Tsh*. Yeah, and I especially need to dangle from a tree limb in the middle of the night for no reason just because I said I'd meet you."

He looks up at me, finally. "Look, I'm sorry I just. I really like, um, being around you and stuff . . . so when I heard that. I dunno. It kinda made me crazy."

But now all of a sudden there's a rustle in the trees and some girl catches us when we're not supposed to be caught. Nobody knows about us, still. And I'm kinda hoping nobody will for a while. I just don't know how to deal with it. How to deal with Becky. It's like a chess game. Too many moving parts.

And then suddenly, out from the trees, there she is.

Stacy Nolan.

Phew. At least it's not *she who shall not be named*.

"Um. Hi."

"Hi Stacy. What's up?"

"Oh, I just . . . I heard somebody back here and . . ."

"Are you walking home?"

"Yeah."

That sucks. That means I'm either gonna have to walk with her or admit, to someone else besides Shelli, that I'm getting moped rides home with Logan. Not good. The more people that know, the sooner Becky finds out.

"Well, I can walk with you, I guess . . ."

"Yeah, yeah. Okay. Cool."

Logan gives me a look. He's not happy about this. But on the other hand, what am I supposed to do? It's not like we're 100 percent together. I mean, we pass secret notes. We've hung out a few times. We've made out like twice. Seriously.

I know you're keeping score, you perv. The fact is so far it's all been basic kissing and a couple of heavy make-out sessions. Logan doesn't seem to be in any big hurry, which is kind of annoying sometimes actually.

Not to mention this whole Jared Kline thing. I mean, yeah, it's true Jared Kline is a scam artist. That is true. But . . . and here's the thing I really don't want to admit to myself: If Jared Kline were madly, passionately, crazily in love with me . . . I'm pretty sure I might have to be in love with him, too, a little bit. Well, okay, a lot. All I know is, when I was in that mahogany office with him . . . it kind of felt like I was in a spaceship or something. I mean, he didn't seem at all like what everybody says. He seemed kind of, I dunno, sweet in a way.

The problem with all of this, of course, is that it's basically a daydream.

I'm not gonna lie to you. I seem to be like the queen of the daydreamers. For instance, at Bunza Hut, when we're just sitting there for eight hours straight staring at our toenails and ringing up French fries, it's kind of like only a matter of time until I start thinking about what it would be like to live in Iceland, or if there is any possibility of marrying a duke, or what about just living someplace really weird in the South Pacific, some island that no one even really knew existed except the locals. Things like that.

You can see why I have to steal just to keep focus.

Right now Logan takes off and Stacy Nolan is walking next to me on the long death march home, in the freezing cold and, frankly, it's a little bit awkward. Neither of us knows what to say, really.

"Hey, so, I wanted to tell you . . ."

"Yeah?"

"I thought that was really nice what you did for me. I mean, not many people would have done something like that. Honestly."

"Well, it wasn't much."

"Yeah, it was. Believe me."

"It wasn't even true, so, I mean, that kind of helped."

"I know!"

We walk on up the hill. It's rows and rows of suburban houses but you can see your breath now. It's obvious my parents are trying to kill me.

"It's kinda weird, right?"

"What? What is?" I'm halfway to daydreaming, she better make it quick.

"Well, I mean, don't you wonder who started that rumor in the first place?"

"Yeah, I guess."

"I sure do."

"Well, let's think. Do you have any enemies or anything?"

"What do you mean?"

"I dunno, did you like do something mean to someone, maybe you didn't even realize until after it was too late or something?"

"Hm. Lemme think."

We walk on and now it's really starting to freeze over. The sun is going down through the scraggly black trees and the leaves on the ground—red, brown, orange—smell burnt. We are about one block past Shelli's house and I can't help but wonder if she's become a born-again Christian yet.

"Anyone? I mean, maybe it was just some dumb thing."

"I dunno. The thing is . . . I'm not like you. I mean, people don't care about me. Like, they don't care what I do. It's like, I dunno, it's like I'm invisible or something."

"Really?"

"Oh yeah. It's like . . . I mean as weird as it sounds, that whole debacle was like the first time half the school even knew I existed."

"No way."

"Yeah. Way."

The fact is, she's telling the truth. And I don't even know why. I don't even know who makes up these unwritten rules about who and what you're supposed to care about. The whole thing seems like throwing spaghetti against the wall. Nobody knows what's gonna stick.

"Well, I knew who you were."

Like that helps. But what else am I supposed to say?

"Thanks. Anyway, you saved my ass, and don't think I'll forget it."

We're walking on and the sun is really starting to take its last bow. The unspoken rule is that I won't invite her to my house and she won't invite me to hers. That's okay, too. It's not like you can be best friends with everybody. Also, she thinks I'm kinda like a good person now and I don't have the heart to let her know that inside I'm spider stew. I better keep her at a distance so she never finds out.

Logan's moped buzzes in the distance and I think . . . I'd feel bad disappointing her.

twenty-four

This dinner is gonna be like the most uncomfortable dinner of my lifetime. Seriously. I don't know what I was thinking.

Of course, my mom thinks this is like the greatest thing ever and that I'm like Mother Teresa or something just for inviting "that black girl" over for dinner. It's weird. It's like somehow I have given my mother the opportunity to care about something for the first time in forever. It's like she's had too much coffee or something.

She's fluttering around the kitchen making this thing and that, putting out this dish and that, asking me to cut this vegetable and that. I mean, I kind of think she's possessed. Even my horrible sisters have noticed. And they are not happy about it. Lizzie, particularly, is livid. This is how the conversation went:

"Mom. Neener and I have a date tonight, so . . ."

"Oh, no no no. Not tonight. Tonight we are having a *very special guest* over for dinner and you are both gonna sit there and be on your best behavior, I mean it."

"Special guest? What is this, *The Tonight Show?*"

"No, honey. Your little sister did something really kind. She reached out to someone, someone who maybe most people wouldn't, and she held out her hand."

I look to the heavens for guidance but see only the kitchen ceiling. "Mother, what is wrong with you?"

"You know what," she continues, "I wish you girls would treat your little sister with more respect, because if you actually opened your eyes . . . you'd see she's a really good person."

But Lizzie is not opening her eyes. She is rolling them.

"Well, what is it, like, a homeless person?"

"No, Lizzie. It's not a homeless person. It's a very lovely girl of African-American descent."

"A black girl?"

"Yes, dear, a black girl."

"Where did she meet a black girl? I thought we didn't have any black people in Nebraska."

"At the Bunza Hut," I mumble.

"Seriously?"

"Yes," my mother chirps. "She goes to Lincoln High, so she's not exactly from 'the right side of the tracks' as they say, but she is a very sweet girl and it's possible her mother is starving her."

Lizzie looks at me. Boy oh boy if looks could kill.

"Little miss perfect strikes again."

Neener doesn't say anything. She just reiterates Lizzie's hatred by standing behind her. If my mom wasn't right there I'd be wrestled to the ground in like two seconds and spit on immediately. But my mom is not having it.

"Now go downstairs please and put on something appropriate for dinner."

"What's wrong with this?"

Lizzie looks at her latest uniform. Jeans and a concert tee over a long thermal underwear shirt.

"What's wrong with that is that we are not going to chop wood, we are going to have a nice dinner here, at a nice table, with our nice china and our best behavior."

"Jesus."

She and Neener go hurtling down the stairs, saying something under their breath to the tune of, "All this for some black girl?"

I stay there and help my mom chop carrots.

"Now, honey, I want you to slice them the long way, and

thin, too, because those are going to be julienne carrots, the secret is the orange juice."

But now we are in trouble because the ogre walks in.

"What's all this?"

"We are having a special guest tonight. Dinner at seven. On the dot."

"Why so late?"

We're talking about a guy who is done with his plate by 6:30 p.m. every night. Just in time for *Wheel of Fortune*.

"Please, just, dinner's at seven."

"Well, who is it?"

"It's a girl from Anika's work."

"From the Bunza Hut? What's so special about that?"

And now Henry comes in, carrying his Trapper Keeper and peeking in to see what's on the stove. Henry never says anything but when he does, it matters.

"She's black."

Now he disappears into his back room for more studies. God, he studies his eyeballs out of his sockets. If he doesn't get into Harvard we are all gonna be on suicide watch.

"You're making all this fuss for a nigger?"

"WADE!"

"Well, doesn't it seem like a lot?"

"Wade, do NOT use that word in this house. I mean it."

"What word?"

"You know what word."

"You mean NNNNN-iiiiiiii—"

"Wade, I mean it. You know how I feel about that. And around the kids!"

He laughs. "Geez, where's your sense of humor?"

He waddles into the kitchen, swings open the cupboard, grabs a bag of Fiddle Faddle, and heads into his master hovel.

"And don't spoil your appetite!"

"Yes, massa!"

He leaves and now it's just Mom and the julienne carrots and me.

"I'm sorry you had to hear that."

"Mom, news flash, he's an idiot."

My mom sighs and shakes it off.

"Okay, now you have to put the butter, before the orange juice."

She takes out a skillet and puts it on the stove. In that moment, I decide a couple of things. One is . . . I'm never cooking for some guy that just grunts and says bad words. And two: The vampire is right. If I don't get straight As I'm gonna get stuck here and if I get stuck here I am gonna kill myself.

twenty-five

Pedaling fast fast fast, this is the moment. This is the moment I'm getting closer and everything is still, everything is still and everything, the trees, the leaves, the sidewalk, everything is holding its breath, waiting.

Pedaling fast fast fast, the trees are leaning in, trying to protect me, trying to grab me, trying to keep me from seeing. The leaves and the sidewalk whooshing by, whispering to each other *don't let her see don't let her see don't let her see.* The stop signs practically begging me, *stop, go back, go home, just go home.*

Pedaling fast fast fast, this is the last moment I get to be this person. This is the last moment before everything changes from pink to purple to black and nothing is ever the same, nothing is ever the same again.

twenty-six

The evening does not go well.

But it's not what you think. The only person who is normal about anything is Tiffany. Everyone else is spazzing out. Especially my mom. But she's spazzing out in a good way, or a nice way, at least. She's kind of acting like the mom on *Leave It to Beaver*. June Cleaver. She's emphasizing everything in the weirdest way possible. Example: "Wade, could you *please* pass the julienne carrots. Thank you *so very* much." Normally this sentence goes like this, "You! Carrots!"

Now, my mom, God bless her heart, is acting this way I don't know why, but I think she's overcompensating, outside of her head, because inside of her head she knows how much no one else at the table is really happy about this after-school-special of a dinner to which their dumb little sister has subjected them.

Like my annoying older sisters, for instance, they are just huddled over to the side of the table like two bitchy bats just waiting for some moment to swoop down and bite out everyone's entrails. My perfect brother, Robby, is the second most normal person. He's eating his food and just waiting for everything to play out with a content but slightly amused smile. This is not surprising because it's sort of the way he deals with everything. One day the Grim Reaper will show up at his doorstep and he'll shrug and say, "Yeah, okay. It's been a good run. Where to?"

Henry is acting pretty weird, honestly. What else is new? Quiet. Check. Brooding. Check. Staring. Check. Now if Robby were acting this way we'd call an ambulance but this is Henry's natural state, so we're all clear.

And what about the ogre, you ask? Well, his way of dealing with this excruciating dinner is to pile his plate as high as possible and stuff his face as fast as possible and not make any eye contact. If he looks up at all, he looks up at my mom, rolls his eyes, and quickly eats another bite of mashed potatoes.

Poor Mom.

"Now, Tiffany, I want to know if they are treating you

girls okay at the Bunza Hut. I try to ask Anika but I can't seem to get a straight answer out of her."

"Mom, what do you think they're doing? It's the Bunza Hut."

Tiffany obliges: "Oh, it's not so bad. They let us drink the shakes."

"Oh, they do, do they?"

"The leftover shakes."

Silence. Confusion.

I chime in to ease everyone's befuddlement: "You have to make the shake in this silver cup thingy, and there's always some leftover. So, we get that."

Now Henry: "But then couldn't you just make the shake bigger?"

"Well, we do. Basically we make the shake twice as big so every time anyone orders a shake we get a free shake." I'm so proud of myself.

"So, you're stealing." That's the ogre. Of course.

Tiffany kind of blushes. Stealing's not her racket. It's mine.

"Well, I just hope you're not abusing that privilege." Mom feels the need to turn this into some kind of life lesson.

"Oh, Mom, the guy's a total jerkface. And he's like superrich. Have you seen their house on Sheridan?! Not to mention he told Shelli she's fat."

Again, Henry: "Their house on Sheridan is worth one million two hundred and seventy-six thousand dollars."

Silence.

Now Robby: "But who's counting."

"Mom, the guy totally sucks. You should see how he talks to Shelli, he just abuses her. It's horrible."

Now the ogre: "Does she work there?"

Now Mom: "Wade—"

"I said, does she *work* there?"

God I hate the ogre. "Yes. She works there."

"So, he's the boss. He can do whatever he wants."

Me: "Nice. That's a nice philosophy. What if he wanted to chop her head off or eat her ankles or something . . . could he do that, too?"

Wade shrugs. Everybody else looks at their plate.

Now the doorbell rings. This is a surprise to everyone but Tiffany.

Mom goes to the door and answers in her best Doris Day.

"Good evening, how may I help you?"

But the person on the other side of the door is not in the mood for Doris Day.

"Tiffany! Get out here right now!"

Of course, now the whole table, our whole table of sibling rivalries, little snickers, and the ogre, turns to look.

Tiffany's mom is not in a good mood. She also looks

like maybe this is the first time she's got out of bed today. Just looking at her, my heart breaks for Tiffany. As meticulous and sweet and orderly as Tiffany is . . . now I see it's maybe a reaction to whatever her mom has going on at home.

"Get out here right now. C'mon now!"

Tiffany is red with shame. God, I wish I could take this from her. And all of us are instantly on Tiffany's side. I can feel it. The whole family, who were so annoyed we had to have this stupid *Leave It to Beaver* dinner . . . well, now we are ready to take Tiffany in as our own.

Come live with us, Tiffany. What's one more? Even the ogre is less ogre-fied. His spine is up. He wants to help. But like all of us, he is helpless.

Mom tries to make it better.

"Would you like to come in for dinner, there's plenty of—"

"Lady, I can take care of my own."

Mom nods. I can tell she's calculating. What can she do? Can she do anything?

"You think I can't take care of my own?"

"No. No. I don't think that. I just thought maybe you might—"

"Well, you thought wrong, lady. C'MON now, Tiffany, I ain't sayin' it again!"

Tiffany ducks out of the dining room and down the stairs and to her mother. Her mother, who moves her, not gently, behind her. We all stare.

"Please, we would love to—"

"Good night." And with that, Tiffany, in her white ankle socks and cute navy skirt, is gone. Back to that cruddy little stucco apartment complex with that just-out-of-bed mom, and the rest of us are just sitting there, struck dumb.

There is a long silence.

Mom comes to the table and starts collecting the plates. Lizzie and Neener look at me. Lizzie does the talking.

"Hey, Anika. That sucks. We didn't know."

"Neither did I, really."

Beat.

Now Neener: "Poor Tiffany."

Now Henry: "I thought she was beautiful."

Silence. Okay, if you were looking for the quietest, weirdest silence in the USA . . . you found it. Right here in this dining room between the oak dining cupboard and the cedar breakfast nook.

Now Robby just starts chuckling. "Well, okay, there you have it."

Now Lizzie and Neener start making funny noises, not a catcall exactly, more like "Ooooo, Henry's in looooooove . . ."

And now it's too much for the ogre.

"DON'T. Don't even think about it, Henry!" He's pointing his finger.

Of course, this makes Lizzie and Neener lose it completely, they are giggling and teasing and snickering it up. Robby's clearing his plate with a smile on his face and Henry is turning the color of a lobster.

"You guys are idiots." Henry clears his plate, shaking his head. "I swear, if I don't get into Harvard I'm going to jump off a bridge." He walks back to his room, annoyed.

"Yeah, a loooooove bridge." Brilliant comment, courtesy of Neener.

The ogre rolls his eyes, gets up, and lumbers back to his room, where he will lie down on his water bed and blast *Wheel of Fortune*, then *The Tonight Show*, then the late-night news.

I say it. "What in the world is a love bridge?"

Mom is just putting away the leftovers. She looks at me, over the Tupperware. She doesn't have to say anything. She just gives me the universal look for "We tried."

We tried what? To have dinner with a black person? To pretend we weren't just a household of generally crappy people? We tried to be less self-involved. We tried to look up from our dumb obsessions and notice other people. We tried to be open, for once. We tried not to be just another vaguely racist family. We tried to be enlightened. We tried to be good.

We tried to be all of the things . . . we are not.

twenty-seven

Today at the Bunza Hut I'm in charge of putting up the Halloween decorations. There're two skeletons, one for each door, and a bunch of pumpkins that I'm assuming will be doing double duty for Thanksgiving. Right now they have faces on them.

Shelli is behind the counter doing her lip liner.

Monday nights are pretty slow because pretty much everybody in Nebraska is addicted to football, thanks to the Cornhuskers, but that translates, of course, to the NFL, so tonight is, basically, a holiday. Sure, people call in big orders to take home and eat in their family rooms, rec rooms, and man caves while they watch the game with the guys but, pretty much, once the game starts, it might as well be the end of days.

Tonight's the Bears vs. Packers. Big matchup. Also, this is a game that shall cleave the heart of the city in twain, as basically Lincoln, Nebraska, is chock-full of both Packers fans AND Bears fans. Yeah, Chicago is closer but that's full of a bunch of city slickers and half the people here are related to people from up north in Wisconsin. Why do you think everyone in this state is blond? They might as well call it *Scandinavia 2: Electric Boogaloo.* Or maybe *Germany 2 . . . This Time, Without Nazis!* There are about five last names at my school: Krauss, Hesse, Schnittgrund, Schroeder, and Berger. It is not unusual to have an uncle named Ingmar.

If you care what I think, I'm a Packers fan. Sorry, everyone else in the world. But really that is just me feeling sorry for you for not being a Packers fan.

These skeletons are not easy to get up. First of all, they're too heavy for this Scotch tape and second of all, these freezing cold glass doors don't seem to want to have anything taped to them. Shelli is not helping.

"I think you should dump that Logan guy."

Shelli always has a way with words.

"How can I dump him? I'm not even going out with him."

"Seriously. What if Becky finds out?"

"Whatever. Wait. How's she gonna find out?"

"I dunno."

"Did you tell her?"

"What? No."

"Shelli, seriously . . . did you tell her?"

"No . . . I didn't."

"Well, don't. Even if she asks or anything."

"I know, I know."

"Can you help me with these stupid skeletons? They won't stay up."

Shelli sighs and comes over, pocketing her lip liner.

So there we are hanging these spooky but not too spooky skeletons on the ice-cold door when it happens.

"Oh my God."

"What?"

"Anika. Oh. My. God."

"Jesus. What?"

"Turn around."

"Seriously. You're scaring me."

"Turn. A. Round."

And so I do. And that's when I see it.

Jared Kline is getting out of his Jeep and walking straight into the Bunza Hut, straight for the door, straight toward us.

"Jesus. Mary. And Joseph. Whaddawedo whaddawedo?!"

"Act cool. Act cool."

Shelli is quivering behind me and I'm not so sure-footed myself.

Jared sees us looking and gives a little wave. Barely a wave. More like a nod from his hand.

The door opens.

"Hey."

"Hey."

Shelli watches in silence as Jared keeps his eyes on me. Her fingernails are bearing into my arms like mini-knives made of the letter C.

"Busy night?"

"Yeah, um . . . I guess everyone's watching the game, so . . ."

"I guess that makes me lucky a little."

Shelli is basically stabbing my arm now with her fingernails.

"So . . . you don't like football . . . ?"

"It's okay." Shrug.

This makes Jared the only guy in Nebraska who doesn't worship at the altar of the pigskin.

"What about you?"

"I dunno. It's fun sometimes, I guess."

"A-ha! Lemme guess . . . you're a Packers fan."

"What . . . how did you know?" I can't help but smile now. I'm busted but Jared is such a stone-cold fox maybe I'm just delirious.

"Because it's kinda like old-school. They're like an old-school team."

"Okay. You got me."

"Do I?"

He's smiling now. This guy is good. He really knows how to make a girl blush.

Shelli elbows me, not so subtle.

"Oh, this is my friend Shelli."

"Hi Shelli."

"Hiii . . ."

Shelli says hi in a really weird way. It's like if you tried to make a deflated balloon speak.

"So, can I order some food or . . . is this just a Halloween decorating operation?"

"Ha-ha, very funny."

And with that we leave Shelli quivering by the door with the skeletons. Now, I'm behind the cash register, kind of wishing I came from one of those households where you didn't have to work. Like Jared.

"You look cute in your little uniform."

Did he read my mind or something?

"Yeah? You don't think I look like an Easter egg?"

"No. I think you look like I should be asking you to marry me."

CRASH!

That was too much for Shelli. She dropped the skeleton, the box of decorations, and the tape. She looks up, mortified. Jared nods, smiling.

"I see this is a dangerous workplace."

"Yeah. Okay, so . . . French fries, or maybe . . . ?"

"I'd like a cheese Bunza. French fries. A Dr Pepper—"

"Oh, you're a Pepper?"

"Yeah. I'm a Pepper. Wouldn't you like to be a Pepper, too?"

I can't help but laugh at this guy. He's actually funny. Kind of a surprise. I thought maybe he'd just be some hot lug-head jerk. But this? This is unfair.

"And a shake."

"Really?"

"Yeah. A shake. Instead of the Dr Pepper. Oh . . . and you. I'd like a date with you. Saturday night."

Holy. Um. Shit.

"That's not really on the menu or whatever."

"I know. That was stupid. I was trying to be clever."

Shelli just so happens to be hanging those decorations closer and closer.

He whispers, "I think your friend is spying on us."

"Well, obviously. You look like a criminal."

He smiles.

"C'mon. Seriously. You're going out with me. Saturday night."

"What? I can't. I've never even been on a date. Like, I

don't even know if my parents will let me."

"What if I talk to them? What if I ask them? What if I come over and respectfully ask your father—"

"He's not my father. He's my stepdad."

"Respectfully ask your stepdad, and your mom, for your hand in a date."

"Oh my God, you're crazy."

But I'm smiling. Mostly I can't even believe this is happening. If Becky were here she would die.

"I think my friend Becky likes you actually . . ."

"Your friend Becky is a horrible person who probably drinks the blood of small children for breakfast."

"Wow. That's fairly accurate."

Shelli is peering out from behind a pumpkin. Her eyes are the size of the pumpkin.

"Okay. That's it. I'm gonna ask your mom. Respectfully. And your stepdad."

"Are you serious? Seriously?"

"I am serious. Seriously."

He walks out, still smiling.

"Hey, wait you forgot your—"

Shelli looks at me from across the Bunza Hut. She's whispering even though it's just us now.

"Anika! Anika!"

"He forgot his food . . ."

"Anika, do you know what this means?!"

"That he's coming back?"

"No. No. It means that . . . I think maybe . . . you're the most popular girl in the school now!"

twenty-eight

Shelli's assessment, that I'm now suddenly bumped up to number one popular girl, is wrong. Way off. But it's nice of her to say it, and flattering.

Really what this means is that Becky, when she finds out, is going to come over to my house, chop my limbs off, feed them into my face, and then chop my head off. I know this the way I know the sky is blue, leaves are green, and sports are boring.

I am attempting to study in my room, which is difficult when you feel dismemberment is in your immediate future.

My mom, in her Mrs. Santa Claus mode, is bringing in milk and cookies. I know exactly what she's gonna say.

"Honey, now don't stay up too late . . ."

I say it with her. She's right. I just have a habit of procrastinating my homework until the absolute last, latest, worst time to possibly do anything.

"Have you heard from Tiffany, honey?"

"Wha? No . . . her shift isn't till Wednesday."

"Oh, well I hope everything's okay."

"Me too, Mom."

She stands there a second.

"Oh! I almost forgot. Someone left something for you . . . wait, hold on . . ."

She scurries out and now I'm really curious. No one's ever left anything for me here before. I don't think anyone even knows exactly where I live.

"Here. It looks like a present, I guess."

It's a tiny box. Black velvet. Wrapped in a little white bow.

My heart gives a thump.

"Well, aren't you gonna open it?"

"I dunno, Mom. Is this from you?"

"No. No, honey. I swear, someone just left it. The boys found it, actually. On the front step."

"That's so weird. Okay, here goes . . ."

I untie the white bow, and lift the little lid.

Wow.

It's a little gold necklace with my name engraved on it in

cursive. Anika. In flowing letters.

"Wow. How cool."

"Wow, you ain't kidding. Here, I'll put it on you."

My mom comes around and clasps it. Now we both look.

"So . . . do you know who it's from?"

"What? Wasn't there a card or something?"

"Nope. It's a mystery."

My mom and I both look in the mirror at the necklace. It's fancy. It's expensive. . . .

"Okay, now, try to go to bed. Will ya? Otherwise I don't feel like I'm doing my job."

"Oh, Mom? Did anybody ever tell you that you're basically like a muffin that got turned into a person?"

Mom smiles and walks to the door. "Oh, that imagination of yours . . ."

"Night, Mom."

"Night, honey."

twenty-nine

The first person to spot the necklace at school is Becky. Of course.

"Nice. Where'd you get it?"

"Oh . . . my mom. She thought—"

"Hunh. That's nice. Is it your birthday or something?"

"No, it's just . . . She said she saw it and she thought of me."

"She saw a necklace that said Anika? What, like, at the Anika store?"

"No, I mean she saw, like, these name necklaces, and she thought of me."

"Oh. Whatever."

Shelli is standing next to me. She knows I'm lying. She can feel it.

"That's awesome, I wish my mom would do something like that . . ."

"Shelli, the only necklace your mom is gonna get you is a dying Jesus."

Becky, as usual, speaks the truth.

My turn. "It's okay, Shelli. I'll buy you a dying Jesus."

Shelli smiles at me. She knows I'm with her. That we're in it together.

"Geez, why don't you guys get a room?"

It drives Becky crazy that Shelli and I are close. She wants to divide and conquer, any way she can. She's deranged.

The bell rings and everyone starts taking off in different directions like crazy and, of course, I run into Logan.

"Did you get the necklace?"

"What?" I glance around and confirm that no one is making note of this encounter.

"Did you get the necklace. I left you a necklace. At your house."

"Oh! Yeah, see, here it is. I'm wearing it."

I don't know why I feel surprised. I guess I wasn't sure it was from Logan?

He looks at me with puppy eyes and I feel like the world's biggest jerk, but I don't know why.

"That was really nice of you. Thank you. Thank you so much."

He smiles. Second bell.

"Gotta go."

He takes off, around the corner and I am left there, standing, late for physics, realizing that I'm the dumbest person on earth because for some insane reason I thought, now don't laugh when you hear this, I thought . . . well, I thought the necklace was from Jared.

thirty

Ladies and gentlemen, I'm confused.

On the one side there's Logan, who, even if he's a social pariah, is really cool and smart and thinks like nobody else I've ever met before. Then, on the other hand, there's Jared Kline, rock star, super-king, and the one person in the world who can protect me from Becky Vilhauer. I mean it's like trying to decide between James Dean and Elvis. Seriously, who could make that choice?

My guilt has led me squarely to the dinner table at Logan's house.

If you were wondering how close Becky lives to Logan McDonough the answer is . . . right across the street. I know. Doomsday scenario. The only good thing is . . . her house is back like a football field from the street because they needed room to put trees, a wall, a fountain, and other stuff to make everybody else feel like shit.

So, even though Becky is almost spitting distance from our little friendly dinner, I'm actually not that scared. And by not that scared I mean, I only checked three times since I've been here to make sure no one has seen me.

Besides, there are other things to be scared of. Like Logan's family. First, there's his mom, who, as far as I can tell, has her cocktail superglued to her fingers. She's a pretty blonde with a huge diamond ring and all. But there's something sad about her. Something resigned. It's like the weight of that huge, shiny rock is pinning her to the ground. Then, there are his two kid brothers, Billy and Lars, who are three and six, respectively. You could cast them in a commercial about cereal, that's how much they look like dumplings. Billy especially, a little towhead with sky-blue eyes.

Then, there's Logan and me.

And, finally, the pièce de résistance . . . Logan's dad.

Logan's dad looks like the kind of guy you are trying to avoid. All smiles and sweaters. Terrifyingly cheerful. And talking. Lots of talking. I mean the guy never shuts up. So far this dinner, which he had catered by the way. I'm not kidding. He ordered out and even had them send over a guy in a white chef's coat to serve us. He must have done this before because the guy in the white chef's coat knows two things: (1) Where the serving plates are, and (2) To keep the wife's drink filled.

I mean, this dinner, here on a Tuesday night, just a regular old Tuesday night, no holidays or anything, must have cost a fortune. Like, my mom's entire grocery budget for the whole month. Apparently this is natural behavior for him. During his monologue about how he's planning on triumphing over the zoning restrictions on his new subdivision, Logan leans in.

"He likes to show off."

Now, Logan's dad doesn't like interruptions.

"What's that, son? You wanna share with the table?"

"I was just telling Anika what a master you are with real estate."

"Oh. So, like I said, we're still waiting on the zone permits. Should be any time now. Goddamn city."

And now Logan's mom actually chimes in.

"Not in front of the boys, please."

There's a silence here.

And now Dad. "You're right. I should spell it out. These F-U-C-K-I-N-G city permits are an F-U-C-K-I-N-G waste of time!"

He slams his drink on the table and, as if on a teeter-totter, as his hand goes down, Logan's mom gets up. She gently wrangles the two little boys, kissing Billy on the head as he wraps around her like a koala. Lars stays close, too, clinging to her leg. She even puts her drink down, miracle, as she scurries the boys upstairs.

Logan looks up at his mom and you can see, now, who he loves most in the world. And he wants to save her from this *thing* at the other end of the table. You can see that, too.

Dad will not be bested. He continues on and on until the end of dinner, even through dessert. Zones, permits, the goddamn bureaucracy, all of it conspiring to ruin his life in paperwork. By the time he leads us down to his man cave in the basement, he's had about six scotches.

The caterers are cleaning up now. Logan's mom has retired to her room, the TV muffled up the stairs. And his two kid brothers, Lars and Billy, waiting upstairs for Logan to tuck them in, which I guess he does each night. Which, honestly? Massive points for Logan.

Downstairs the man of the house sure is proud of his gun cupboard or whatever you call it. Display case, I guess. My mom would freak her eyeballs out if she even saw me in this room. No joke.

Meanwhile, Logan's dad is pointing at each of his prize possessions, a litany of names that all sound vaguely menacing, conquering, and are all, obviously, invented deep in the recesses of the gun manufacturers' board rooms where a panel of guys probably sits around throwing out names that will make guys feel like they have bigger penises.

Logan is totally embarrassed by his dad, who boasts about each and every gun, its name, and what type of animal he killed with it.

Oh, I didn't mention the insane amount of deer, geese, and wild boar "trophies" he has displayed in his man cave? Let me tell you . . . I started counting five minutes ago and lost track. That's how many.

Right now he's showing me a gun that I think I saw in that movie *Rambo*.

"See, this one here's a beaut. Bushmaster AR-15 semiautomatic rifle. You wanna hold it?"

"Dad—"

"I am asking your friend, thank you."

"Um, no, sir. No thanks."

"Your loss. Wanna see something else?"

He is about to pull another gun out of the cabinet when Logan starts again.

"Okay, Dad, we really gotta—"

And it happens so fast. It happens before I even knew it could happen and before I can believe it.

Logan's dad backhands him on the cheek so hard it leaves a welt.

Silence.

Upstairs the caterers clink and clank the silverware but down here there is only silence.

Logan's dad looks at him, that drunk-eyed look of a dare. *Dare you to fight back, son. Wanna fight back?*

He breathes hard. "I *said* I was addressing your friend."

There's nothing to say. I mean, there's a million things to say but I can't say one of them.

Logan looks up, his hand on his cheek. The welt from his jaw to his ear.

"Thanks, Dad. You always knew how to leave a good impression."

Logan heads upstairs, and I don't blame him.

Now it's just me and Rambo over here.

"Excuse my son, Anika. His mother wasn't successful in teaching him manners."

"I-I, uh—"

"But I bet you understand why a man would be proud of this kind of collection," he steamrolls on. "Just look at it! Do you know how much care and expense is contained in this case?"

I nod, then: "I'm sorry, Mr. McDonough, but I need to be home in time for curfew."

And with that he smiles, picks up that ridiculous cartoon gun, and I do believe that's my exit. Yes, this is definitely my exit.

I make my way up the stairs with the world's most uncomfortable smile. No fast moves. At the top of the stairs, I look back at good ol' dad. He's sitting there on his stool with his scotch and his Bushmaster. PS: Nice name—Bushmaster. I guess that gun makes him "master of the bush."

He is smiling to himself, a dull smile, unfocused. His eyes glazed over. It almost seems like he's talking to himself but nothing's coming out. Whatever it is, I'll bet you a shiny nickel it is some sort of paranoid rant about the government, freedom, our forefathers, and how someday he's gonna save the world.

So. I guess Logan has me beat on the bad dad front.

He's at the top of the stairs, waiting for me.

"Sorry, Anika."

"What?! *You're sorry?* No. I'm fucking . . . I don't even know what to—"

"Yeah. Kind of like a car crash."

We make our way up to the second floor. There's two sets of stairs up here, one for the "servants" I guess, and one for the people who are supposed to be important. I wait there on the servants' steps while Logan goes to tuck Billy and Lars into bed for the night. I'm terrified his dad is gonna come lumbering up the important-people stairs with that stupid small-penis gun. Luckily, these steps offer a kind of shelter. I mean, not much but at least it's something. His mom is hiding, too. Her door is closed, the blue light of the TV coming out under it.

I can see why she keeps that cocktail full, let me tell you. I probably would, too, married to that freak.

If I peek in I can see Logan turning on their little night-light, a mini Yoda that matches the *Star Wars* sheets and Billy's R2-D2 socks. Billy doesn't want to give back his dinosaur but Logan explains it has to protect him from the foot of the bed. Billy sees the logic in this and relents.

"See, your dinosaur will protect you. Rawr!"

"It's an ankylosaurus."

"Oh, okay. Your ankylosaurus will protect you."

"Can I have my T. rex, too?"

"Yes, of course. You need your T. rex and your ankylosaurus. They're in cahoots."

That's one smart three-year-old, I've gotta say. I'm not sure I could've said ankylosaurus, let alone recognized one, at that age. They're such cute little boys, Billy with his towhead and Lars in his Spider-Man footy sleeper. Their room is full of everything little boys love. Trains. Dinosaurs. Trucks. The *Millennium Falcon* and the Death

Star poised for battle on the shelf.

Looking at Logan in there, tucking them in and giving them each a peck on the forehead, I can't help but think that I'm an idiot and that he may be, quite possibly, the greatest guy in the world.

thirty-one

By the time I get to work on Wednesday it's total drama. I walk in and Shelli nods her head in the direction of the back, giving me the universal look for The Shit Has Hit the Fan. I go through to find Tiffany in the back with the manager and two cops.

Cops? What the—?

"Anika, not now. We have a situation."

Tiffany can barely glance up at me. She looks stricken, you can tell she's been crying.

"What's going on? What is this?"

"Well, if you must know . . . Tiffany here has been stealing."

It hits me like a sledgehammer.

Oh, no. All this time I've been stealing their faces off and now they think it's Tiffany! Because she's black. It's that simple.

"No, she hasn't!"

Mr. Baum scoffs. "Um, Anika? I think I know when the drops are short."

Tiffany, on the gray plastic seat in the corner, looks like she's in pain. God, this is excruciating! I'm gonna have to come clean. I'm gonna have to turn myself in. I'm gonna have to ruin my college transcripts. Christ. The Count is going to draw and quarter me. Then he is going to feed my body to the vultures. Then he is going to draw and quarter the vultures.

"No. Listen. It wasn't her, I swear—"

"Anika, shhh!"

And then he plays the tape. The ongoing video they have on the cash register. And the cops see it and Tiffany sees it and I see it.

There on the video is Tiffany, indeed, stealing out of the cash register.

No plan, no system, nothing.

Just plain stealing.

I can't believe it. I can't believe my eyes.

Tiffany looks up at me, her cheeks on fire. I can tell she's totally ashamed.

She mouths the words "I'm sorry."

I mouth back, "It's okay."

And I want to tell her we've been stealing their pants off for the past six weeks and that's why they even thought to look at the tapes, so it's my fault, which it is, by the way. This is all my fault.

"Sir, do you wish to press charges?"

"Damn straight."

Ugh. What an asshole. I have to do something.

"No, wait! I made her do it!"

"Excuse me?"

"Yeah, I put her up to it. It was stupid and I was to blame."

"Listen, Anika, that's nice of you but—"

"Mr. Baum, I told her to do it! I told her if she didn't I'd get her fired. It was stupid and immature and I don't even know what I was thinking but she didn't want to do it. I swear. She begged me."

Mr. Baum looks at me, still unconvinced.

"That's not like you, Anika."

"I know. I told her it was like an initiation. I was being a jerk. I don't know what I was thinking."

"Is this true, Tiffany?"

Tiffany looks at me for permission. I nod, as slight as can be.

"Yes, sir."

"Anika made you?"

"Yes, sir."

"Why didn't you tell us?"

"I didn't want to get her in trouble."

"Well, she sure as shit got you in trouble."

Tiffany nods. The cops whisper something to Mr. Baum. I can see Tiffany behind them. We make eye contact.

She mouths again, "Thank you."

I wink.

But that doesn't mean I'm not busted. I'm in trouble now and my mom is gonna kill me. I'll probably be fired. Oh, well. It's not like my dream is to be the ruler of the Bunza Hut—

"Tiffany, you're fired."

"What?" I yelp. "But she didn't do anything!"

"Anika, stay out of this. You've done enough, don't you think?

"Please, Tiffany, get your things and call your mom. It's time to go. That's it."

"Mr. Baum, please—"

"And you. We're gonna have a talk. Come with me."

Ugh. Why did I come to work today? Why did I even take this stupid job? And even worse. Why did I steal? I mean, what was I thinking? Of course Mr. Baum would press charges if he knew. He's a mean little man, taking it out on the world.

Now he's dragged me into the storage room. It's just the two of us and the Bunza Hut inventory.

"Anika. I know you're lying."

"What?"

"I know you're lying to cover for that girl."

"No, I'm not."

"It's okay. You're a good person."

"You're not firing me?"

"What? No. You're our best worker."

I gulp. God, talk about totally unfair. If only he knew . . .

"I'd like to give you a raise."

I really should stop poisoning him with Valium. It is clearly affecting the decision-making areas of his brain.

"Mr. Baum, you don't—"

"Just stop it. Christmas is coming, maybe you could buy something—"

"Do you really have to fire her?"

"Yes, Anika. I do. These people need to know—"

"These people?"

"You know."

"Unh. Mr. Baum, just because she's—"

"Anika. Sometimes stereotypes exist for a reason." He pauses. "Look. You're young. You don't know anything yet. Someday you'll get it. Now get back to work. Shelli's probably crashed the register by now."

I don't know what to say to any of this. All I know is I'm the worst person on earth. Worse than the lowest amoeba on the lowest worm to crawl around the lowest swamp on earth.

I get back to the register and Shelli sidles up to me, close enough to whisper.

"What happened?"

"They fired Tiffany."

Shelli's saucer eyes turn to plates.

"For what?!"

"Stealing."

Shelli looks at me. She knows we're to blame. She doesn't know what to think. I can see the gears officially grind to a stop in her head.

"They caught her on tape."

"What? They did?"

"Yup. I saw it."

"So it wasn't—"

"No. It wasn't."

"Phew. I feel better."

"Wull, I don't because they probably wouldn't have noticed if it wasn't for us."

"Oh."

"I think our stealing careers are over, Shelli."

Through the Halloween decorations, out the glass doors I can see Tiffany's mom drive up fast and slam on the brakes. Not happy. Tiffany gets in and it's all I can do not to run out there and pull her out and tell her just to go to my house, go to my mom, join our family. It's not her fault. None of this is her fault. It's my fault. All of it. And I know it.

thirty-two

It's twenty-two degrees out and Mom's driving me home after my shift. It's dark already and outside you can see your breath.

"Mom, do you believe in Jesus?"

"What, honey?"

"Do you believe in Jesus? Like he was the son of God and he did all those magic tricks and then flew up to Heaven in the three days or whatever."

"I dunno, honey. Jury's out."

We drive on in sacrilege.

"But, one thing is for sure, Anika. What goes around comes around."

Uh-oh. That is not a message I am trying to hear.

"How was work, honey?"

"Oh, you know . . ."

"Slow shift?"

"Mom, they fired Tiffany."

"What?! Why?"

"For stealing."

We're almost home and none too soon. I hate the cold.
Even inside the car your feet are freezing, your toes like mini
icicles.

"But how do they—?"

"They had it on video."

"Oh, that's awful. Just awful."

"I know. Mr. Baum obviously thinks it's 'cause she's
black."

"Hm."

"Mom. It's not 'cause she's black, it's 'cause she's poor. I'd
steal, too, if I was in her shoes."

"No, you wouldn't."

"Mom, a lot of people steal. A lot. People who aren't even
poor."

Now we're stopped in the driveway.

"Like who?"

"I dunno. Just people."

"Well, what people?"

"Forget it."

"Like you?"

"What? No."

"Listen. I'm not saying you are, or you have. I'm not saying that. But if you are, or you have, you better stop, immediately, and I mean it. Hypothetically."

"Mo-om."

"You want someone to press charges? You wanna ruin your college transcripts? You wanna be stuck here for the rest of your life?"

"No."

"Okay. Well, then, don't even think about it. I mean it . . . Okay, honey? That's not you. Okay? That's not how I raised you."

But she's wrong. Even though she did everything a mom could do to make me peach pie, inside I'm still spider stew. I'll always be spider stew. I'll spend the rest of my life pretending I'm not and that I'm candy corn and candy cane and candy apple but inside, inside . . . well, you might as well just dip a tarantula in chocolate and call it a day.

thirty-three

The perfect thing about a Wednesday night is no one thinks you're going anywhere. It's like the March of the week, nothing doing. Logan is waiting outside on the corner and I am doing my hot acrobatic sneak-out moves to get out this window and down this tree before my sisters hear me and blow the whistle. Boy, they would love that.

You might as well draw a heart around Logan, standing there in the moonlight with his moped and vaguely surly brow. By the time he hands me his helmet I have completely forgotten about Tiffany and the money and the fact that I'm obviously going to jail.

Flying down our ticky-tacky street to Holmes Lake, there's not a soul around for miles. Nobody's supposed to be at Holmes Lake at one in the morning. This is a family town, see? These paddleboats and bike paths are strictly meant for people in sunscreen. We have to sneak into a hole in the fence about half a mile from the boathouse. This park is all about the lake, and the park is about three miles wide. This is like a big city attraction and even though it's right by our house, we never seem to get here as a family. I think because there's no TV.

Tiptoeing through in the dark, to the boathouse, it feels like we could potentially run into a serial killer, a brigade of the undead, or maybe just a run-of-the-mill ax murderer. Logan is holding my hand, the moped left behind. He's got a backpack on so I am guessing he has some sort of plan here.

You can see the stars reflecting off the lake, still as ice and probably just as cold. It's pitch-black out here and I'm betting, on occasion, more than one person has walked right into the lake. The boathouse is a one-story wooden box, basically, locked but that doesn't seem to be stopping Logan from jimmying the lock with a pin.

"Um. Are you a CIA agent?"

"Yes. This is the first thing they teach us in spy school."

He gets the lock on the third try and next thing I know, he's in the little boathouse.

"Stay out here, just for a second."

Okay, that's annoying because I'm starting to freeze my mittens off. The sound of the rowboats, clacking into the dock, is only about the second spookiest sound on earth. The dock goes out about fifty feet into the lake; all along it the little rowboats are tethered, like leaves on a tree.

"Okay, okay, ready?"

"Um. Yeah."

"Okay . . . ta-dah!"

I look in and it's not exactly the Ritz or whatever but I gotta hand it to Logan. He gets an A for effort. There's about five lanterns around the room, you know, the kind you always see weather-faced lighthouse keepers holding in paintings, with oil and whatever else is involved in making a continuous fire that doesn't burn your ears off. There's a little table in the middle of the room with a lantern in the middle and some kind of picnic—grapes, cheese, beer. You may think this seems like just some low-rent scam but Logan seems pretty proud of it and, if you saw the look in his eyes, you would want to run off with him by dawn, even to Oklahoma.

"Wow. I dunno what to say . . ."

"Why say anything? You don't have to . . ."

"Okay."

He pulls out a wooden chair for me and I sit, suddenly feeling embarrassed, or worried, or like something is gonna go wrong and he's gonna realize I'm not worth all of this after all.

"What's wrong?"

"I dunno. I guess. I just want you to like me."

"I do like you. Why do you think I did all this?"

"I know, but it's like . . . I want you to stay liking me, you know?"

"So you're like worried about something that's not happening . . . ?"

"Yeah, kinda."

The boats outside sway into the dock, creaking.

"You know, Anika. You could waste your whole life worrying, you know that?"

"What do you mean?"

"Well, what if you look back one day and you're like, 'FUCK . . . all I did was worry . . . for the past eighty years—'"

"I guess."

"Look, you don't have to get an A plus right now, or be cool, or anything. You just have to be here with me."

I sort of don't know what to say to this. Except that it is perfect.

And I'm looking at him and it's like he's the hero, but a dark kind of hero, and I'm the ingenue and any second now he's gonna sweep me off my feet and the movie music is gonna swell and "THE END" is gonna get spelled out in cursive on the screen, before the credits roll.

He leans in and we are just about to kiss and there are just about to be fireworks and the orchestra is just about to play.

Except.

There's a noise outside, creaks on the dock, not the sound of the rowboats tethered. The sound of footsteps.

So now the movie music stops and the projector runs out and the screen goes white and the theater lights go up and the audience grumbles, cheated.

Those footsteps are heavy and getting closer.

"Hey! Who's that in there? Git outta there! Come on out."

This is not a nice voice. And not a city voice either. This is the voice of someone who comes from a shack somewhere out in the sticks.

Logan motions me to be quiet, standing at the door.

"Can I help you?"

"Yes, you can help me. I'm the goddamn security and you can help the goddamn security by getting the hell outta there."

"You got a deal, sir. Just leave me be and I'll go on home. I promise."

"I said git and I meant it."

"I mean it, too, sir. Just gimme two seconds—"

But the door's open and there he is.

This guy's got a red face, red hair, and freckles. He might as well be a representative for the color red. He's got a parka on, work boots, and I can smell him all the way from the table. Whiskey. I guess I don't blame him. What else is he supposed to do wandering around Holmes Lake each night with no one to talk to but the lampposts.

He's also representing Hair Growing in Weird Places. Like out of his ears. And his nose. I'm surprised he doesn't have hair growing out of his eyeballs, to be honest. The only place he's not growing mutant hairs is his mouth. That's because his mouth is representing spit, lots of it, coming out the corners. A ravished mouth on a red-faced troll in a parka.

I'd swear this guy is on the run from county but he's got the Holmes Lake logo on that parka, so he gets to boss us around.

Then he sees me and something changes. Now he looks around the room at the lanterns and the picnic and he whistles.

"Well, well. Looks like we got a bit of romance here . . ."

Logan steps in front of him, sheltering, trying to block my view.

"We'll be out of here now, don't worry."

"Oh, I'm not worried. Not anymore."

Logan's shoulders bristle from behind.

"I said we're leaving."

"Okay. Have at it."

He stands at the door, keeping guard as Logan and I scurry to get the fuck out of this hairy troll's boathouse. You would think we were actual spiders the way we've got all arms reaching and packing and bundling to get outta there before whatever this is in the air, mean and sinister, comes to pass.

We duck out the door past whiskey-breath and that's all easy-peasy except that whiskey-breath decides to try out some poetry on me.

"That's a sweet little snatch you got there."

He says it and before it finishes or before it hits me or before I can get those words off me, Logan's got a wooden oar to his head. It lands him square in the face and he hits the dock with a thud.

I am running before he can get up and it's obvious to me that Logan is running right next to me, up the hill and back through the fence, except I hear that oar going *crack, crack, crack* and I look back and Logan isn't anywhere near me, not even close. No, Logan is back at the dock, right where he was, raising that oar up and down, up and down again with the force of a battle-ax. And that guy is representing the color red, alright, but now the color is a deep red, a brick red, that he's representing down his face, down his ears, down his neck, down into the cedar of the docks, down deep into the wooden planks and into the water below.

I mean, the guy can barely move. The guy can barely do anything besides loll in pain, swaying back and forth on his knees making a noise that sounds like begging.

And you would think that Logan would be satisfied with a half-dead troll rolling around at his feet like a flailing fish but he keeps going.

He keeps going.

"Stop it!! STOP IT! WHAT THE FUCK?! STOP!" It's my voice, but the words are just spilling out of me, out of my control.

It's my voice but it might as well be on mute 'cause Logan doesn't hear me. He doesn't hear me, and he doesn't stop until the man is lying there facedown on the dock, a fish gilled.

Logan looks at the man, losing steam, and throws the oar in the water.

He looks up at me.

Jesus.

The man is writhing on the dock, barely, a dull moan but thank God he's alive.

Logan starts up the hill toward me and I don't know what to do. What the fuck am I supposed to do? Am I supposed to run? Am I supposed to fall in his arms, kiss him, and say *my hero*? What the fuck am I supposed to do with whiskey-breath pummeled and he's pummeled for me?

I take off through the trees, trying to make the fence before Logan, trying to see if maybe there's a way home, maybe it'll be a longer walk but maybe that's what I deserve or something.

I hear Logan behind me, running up the hill now, trying to catch up.

"Anika!"

There are about a billion things I could say but I think the best way to say them is to just get lost and let that be that. I mean, seriously, what if that guy dies or something? And worse, it didn't even seem to register for Logan—what he was doing. How awful it was.

Like that quick backhand to the cheek in the basement.

Like his dad.

I mean, even the ogre, who has decided to make a career out of ignoring me and making me feel like a parasite on the belly of a barnacle, would never, ever, do something like that. It wouldn't even occur to him. Maybe more popcorn and more *Wheel of Fortune* but never a backhand slap that makes a welt right then and there.

And it would never occur to me.

But to Logan, it has occurred.

It not only has occurred, but it has manifested. It's manifested in an eviscerated whiskey fish lying prone on the dock, moaning.

And you gotta wonder. If it manifested in that . . . what else could it manifest in? What other things does this person, this person who I thought I knew, who I thought was gentle, who I thought was kind and erudite and sophisticated, this Logan who I almost just kissed in that movie moment and who I thought I was maybe kinda in love with . . . what else does he have up his sleeve?

The fence isn't coming fast enough and I'm running out of breath.

"Anika! Come on!"

He's caught up with me now and I can't even look at him.

"Anika. Stop it. Okay? I'm here. It's me, okay?"

We are both out of breath and our breath is coming out like smokestacks in the cold.

I turn to walk toward the fence. For once in my life I have no idea what to say or to think or to do.

"Anika, I'm sorry. I just . . . I was being protective, okay?"

"That was not protective. That was insane."

"C'mon—"

"You almost killed him."

"Anika, I didn't mean—"

"Look, I know that guy was a creep and, trust me, that

was really gross but . . . *what the fuck just happened?*"

"Okay, I know. I know. You're right. What can I say? That guy, I mean, if he woulda laid a finger on you . . ."

"But he didn't. Okay. He didn't."

"I know. I told you. I lost it, okay? I fucking lost it. Because he said that shit to you."

We both just stand there, catching our breath, the stars not noticing us.

"I want you to take me home now. I just wanna go home, okay?"

"Okay." He looks at me with the eyes of a puppy that's just been scolded for chewing the newspaper. And I want to hold him, to tell him that it's okay.

But okay is not exactly what it is.

We don't say anything the rest of the way through the trees, or through the fence, or through the streets of a place with no people for miles. We don't say anything when I hop off his moped and hand him his helmet and walk up to the tree below my window and don't look back.

thirty-four

If you show up at dinner at my house, that's already front-page news. That's a headline. And nobody thought there would be headlines tonight. It's just a dumb Thursday with Mexican casserole and some leftovers from earlier in the week. Tomorrow will be fish sticks. Monday night my mom is making steak, she said, which I think is totally disgusting but the ogre thinks is top-shelf. If you live in Nebraska, eating steak is the equivalent of eating oranges in Florida. Steak is everywhere. The whole state is steak. We might as well have a T-bone on our state flag.

I know, I know, everywhere else it's a delicacy or something. It means big times. Here . . . it means it's a Monday and nobody cares.

But tonight is kind of a low-level night, nothing doing. And, after last night, and the great boathouse caper, I'm grateful. Nope, tonight even my sisters are up to nothing. Robby's at football practice. The Knights play the Spartans this weekend. Big game. For high school. Everybody will go to that game, even if they don't watch it. It's just what you do on Friday nights in Lincoln. Like birds fly south for the winter. Jenny Schnittgrund will be there, newly tanned. Charlie Russell will be there, with a new rugby shirt. The pep squad girls will be there, freezing on the bleachers in their miniskirts, dreaming of their future glory as cheerleaders. *Oh, one day, one day, to be a real live cheerleader!* We all go, in droves, to the Friday night football game and walk around and giggle and freeze our jeans off and, afterward, everybody marches over to Valentino's Pizza Parlor. It's like a religion or something.

To stay home? To not go to the game? Whoa. That's like anarchy.

(If you want to know how authentic the food is at Valentino's, just remember that the waitresses pronounce it "EYE-talian.")

But tonight at Chez My House, everyone is just clanking and clattering their silverware and shoveling Mexican casserole into their mouths. And then it happens.

Ding-dong.

We look up.

Ding-dong. Ding-dong-ding.

We freeze. It's like we're guilty or something. Maybe we are busted for being too boring.

My mom goes to the door.

"Hello, may I help you?"

"Yes. Yes, ma'am. Hi there. Sorry to bother you. I'm Jared. Jared Kline. Nice to meet you."

The table might as well be an ice sculpture now. We are frozen. We are terrified. We are waiting.

My sisters, who both went to school with Jared and who both worship the ground Jared walks on, like every other girl in the city, look at each other. Me? Is he here for me? I mean, it might as well be Ed McMahon out there with balloons and a Publishers Clearing House sweepstakes check for a zillion dollars.

"Hello, Jared. Nice to meet you, too. As you can see, we're in the middle of dinner, so what can I do for you?"

"Yes, ma'am. Sorry, ma'am. I was just wondering if I could take your daughter out on a date, Saturday night. If I could have your permission?"

Lizzie and Neener are basically both having a heart attack at this point. I can see them planning their outfits, wondering which one he's gonna ask. They will slit each other's throats to go on this date.

Henry looks up, pondering. This is a social science experiment he finds intriguing.

"My daughter?"

"Yes, ma'am . . . your daughter . . ."

If the whole house could lean in, so as to get a closer listen, it would. What was that, sonny?

"Your daughter . . . Anika."

Oh my God, you should see Lizzie's face. She is about to rush me with the butter knife.

Henry tilts his head to the side. This is a new development. An interesting one. The ogre pretends not to listen. Just leave him the rest of the Mexican casserole and he'll be fine.

"Anika. You would like to take *Anika* on a date."

"Yes, ma'am. With your permission."

My mom looks back at me, a question mark.

This is the part where I am supposed to blurt out, "No! No! I love Logan! I belong to Logan McDonough and he is mine and we'll be together forevermore!"

Except I don't do that.

In fact, I do the opposite of that.

I nod.

My head nodded. I didn't nod. But my head nodded.

My head has obviously been taken over by witches.

"And where do you propose to go on this date?"

"Well, ma'am. There's a Halloween festival thing downtown. Like with scary rides and a haunted house and stuff."

"Huh. Is there a hayride by any chance . . . ?"

"No, ma'am. No hayride."

"Because I'm not letting my daughter go on any hayrides with strange boys . . ."

"No, ma'am. I would never. I . . . I just thought the haunted house might be fun, and the scary rides . . . but if it's not we could do something else, go see a movie or—"

"Close that goddamn door!"

Thanks, ogre. You really have a way with words.

Jared peeks in and sees the ogre. He catches my eye. And keeps it. He gives me a wink.

My sisters fantasize about cutting me up and adding me to the Mexican casserole. No one knows what's in there anyway.

"Well, Jared. Looks like you have yourself a date. Good night."

And with that my mom shuts the door on Jared Kline.

She comes back to the table. Puts her napkin on her lap. Somehow this whole event has made her smile like the cat that ate the canary. Who knows why? Moms. Sometimes they seem so silly and worrying and hilarious but sometimes you get the feeling they know everything.

"Who was that, dear? Do you at least know that boy?"

"Yeah."

"Tsh." My sisters scoff. They're pissed. They want me dead.

I make a personal note to duck out after dinner and lock my door before they catch up with me, pin me down, and spit in my mouth. That's Lizzie's favorite. She's demonic. And worse, now she's pissed.

"So, you *do* know him?"

"Yeah."

"Know him?" Now Henry chimes in, having observed the social experiment. "Mother, he's essentially the most popular guy in Lincoln, and possibly Omaha. It would be equivalent to Bruce Willis showing up to ask you out."

At this, the ogre grunts. Out of jealousy? Is he actually jealous of the hypothetical situation my brother has posed?

"Well. If Bruce Willis came round and asked me out I'd tell him I'm married, thank you very much."

"Oh, Mom. What a crock!"

We all chime in. My sisters throw their napkins at her and we all start giggling.

"I would! I would, I tell you!"

"Yeah, Mom, and I would turn into a pumpkin if Matt Dillon asked me out."

"Yeah, Mom. If Madonna asked me out, I'd tell her to fuck off!"

At this, we all burst out laughing. Except the ogre. He's super-pissed Henry used the f-word but that's just making everything even more hilarious and none of us can stop laughing now and making each other laugh at our laughs and even my mom is laughing. Really laughing. And that, in itself, makes it worth it.

thirty-five

Today is the big day of the super-lame, this-totally-sucks six-hundred-yard dash. Mr. Dushane, aka "Dush-nozzle," has made it pretty obvious this is do-or-die time for little old me.

He's giving some speech about never giving up and he keeps looking over at me. Either he has tailor-made this speech for yours truly or he has a crush on me. But I doubt it. He's always drooling over Jenny Schnittgrund. Guess he's a sucker for too much mascara and orange skin.

Shelli doesn't give a shit if she gets a B in this class, or a C or an F, for that matter. Her mom doesn't care. Nothing matters because Christ is saving them all anyway so what's the point? She might as well just sit at home eating bonbons and watching *Hogan's Heroes*.

But not me. No.

I have to care.

I have to care because if I get a B in this class either the vampire will come and fetch me out of this school and send me to study under the Catholic Jesuits in a Romanian nunnery, or . . . or . . . I will be damned to a life eating Cheetos in a double-wide with a husband named Bubba and nine kids who look like extras from *Mad Max*. We'll be poor but we'll have love. And guns.

What Mr. Dushane is not counting on is my thespian abilities. This is my plan.

First, start out the race, seeming inspired by his heart-warming speech.

Second, near the four-hundred-yard mark, begin to pant, begin to lose faith, begin to doubt the existence of God.

Also, drool.

Drooling is not hard to do. All you have to do is think of a lemon.

Try it.

I'll wait.

. . .

See. I told you.

Okay, third. The pièce de résistance.

While drooling, and swaying like a rookie on Mount Everest, running out of oxygen and wobbling around with altitude sickness . . . I will look up at Mr. Dushane.

I will look up at Mr. Dushane, because I know he will be looking over at me and wondering if his speech mattered or if the world is just a meaningless place consisting of an endless series of gestures signifying nothing.

I will hyperventilate.

I will practically fall to the ground.

I will cry.

But then . . . then, folks, I will look up at the you-can-do-it eyeballs of Mr. Dushane and I will be heartened, nay, inspired. I will suddenly feel a sense of power, hope, and the triumph of the human spirit. Glory will wash over me.

No, my legs will not give out!

Not here! Not now!

Not with Mr. Dushane and his dumb speech!

Today is the day that Mr. Dushane saved me!

Today is the day that Mr. Dushane changed a life.

Today is the day that Mr. Dushane mattered.

Except that, by the five hundredth yard . . . the one where the triumph of the human spirit has overtaken me, I hit the ground with a thud and black out.

thirty-six

Yeah, I probably should have trained.

I mean, it's one thing to put on the grand theatrics, but it's another thing entirely to actually do the work. Which, apparently, I never thought of.

Mr. Dushane is standing above me. As is Shelli, Jenny Schnittgrund, and Charlie Russell. There is grave concern.

"Anika, Anika, can you hear me . . . ?"

"Anika, don't go into the light!"

(That's gotta be Shelli.)

Suddenly, the blurry circles around me turn into heads and Mr. Dushane is stooped over me like a terrified turtle.

"Anika. Are you okay? What day is this?"

Oh, this is gonna be fun. . . .

"Wha? What . . . ? Apple."

Mr. Dushane panics. He turns the kids away. This is too important for Charlie, Shelli, or the Oompa-Loompa. He can't have witnesses.

"Anika. What month is it? Do you know what month it is . . . ?"

I wait. I look at him.

"Taco?"

Mr. Dushane is officially losing his shit.

"Anika, I want you to think. I want you to really think. Where are we? What state do we live in . . . Can you remember what state . . . ?"

Pause.

"Cleveland."

Now Mr. Dushane is practically crying. I am not kidding. He is seeing his bank account shrink, his house full of moving boxes, and his wife leaving him for the Realtor. Okay, I can't take it. The guy's a dick, but even I am not that diabolical.

"It's Nebraska. We're in Nebraska."

"That's right! We're in Nebraska!"

Never has anyone been that excited to say that sentence in American history.

"And you're Mr. Dushane. And there's Shelli . . . and Charlie . . . and Jenny . . ."

I'm just copying the end of *The Wizard of Oz*, here, by the way. Just straight up plagiarizing.

"That's right, Anika. We're all here. We're all here for you, okay?"

I can see Shelli over Mr. Dushane's shoulders and she knows exactly what I'm up to. She knows me. She knows and she is doing everything in her power to keep from laughing.

"Mr. Dushane, did I finish . . . ? Did I finish the six-hundred-yard dash?!"

I might as well be asking if I saved the world. If I thwarted the Nazis. If we won State.

"Please, Mr. Dushane. Please . . . tell me the truth . . ."

"Um. Anika. I'm afraid you didn't finish. You passed out."

"I can do it! Out of my way!"

And with this, I attempt a measly, totally pathetic attempt to rise to my feet.

"No, Anika, NO!"

Mr. Dushane thwarts my noble plan and sets me back down, gently.

"Anika. You don't have to. You've done enough."

And now it's speech time. Now he's playing to the class.

"I think we've all learned something here today."

Oh my God, you should see Shelli's face.

"I think Anika has proved to all of us that you never give

up, no matter what . . . No. Matter. What."

The class is looking on, completely apathetic.

"And you know what, Anika. I'm gonna remember this. I'm gonna remember that today . . . today, *you* were the teacher."

It's really hard for me to keep a straight face at this particular moment.

Mr. Dushane helps me to my feet and walks me over to the bleachers.

I did it. Not exactly the way I had it planned but . . . I did it.

I made him feel important.

And walking back to the locker room with Shelli by my side, I can't help but wonder . . . if it's such a big deal for a middle-aged white guy to feel important . . .

What happens when he doesn't?

thirty-seven

Friday night at the Bunza Hut equals ghost town. I mean, I could turn into a frog in here and no one would even notice. Six p.m. and only one customer in three hours. And that lady just asked to use the restroom.

No one wants to work now because of the big game. Mr. Baum thinks I'm such a hard worker because I always offer to take this shift but really it's just so I can get out of going to the game without people thinking I'm a communist.

I'm boning up on my AP English. We're reading this book now about this boy that gets kicked out of boarding school and he doesn't really seem to care about anything. I get it. I'm crossing my fingers that nobody comes in now so I can make it to the end. Only thirty pages left.

I've been avoiding Logan since the boathouse incident. I mean, what am I supposed to do? It's not like I don't miss him or anything. I do. Like, I miss the way he slumps his shoulders and hides behind trees and stuff. But I'm also freaked the fuck out. I've been checking the papers and nothing about the incident. Thank God. Kind of makes me wonder if the whole thing wasn't some weird dream. Like maybe I just made it up and I don't have to think about that whiskey-breath ever again.

On the other hand, I can't help but think of Logan's psycho dad and that makes me feel two things at once. The first is . . . I feel for Logan. Think about it. You gotta figure that wasn't the first time the dad slapped him around. And talk about protective? That look he gave his mom? You have to figure Logan's running interference for her and his two kid brothers on a constant basis. Like he's the hero of the house, in a way. But on the other hand, maybe he's also gonna be just as much of a psycho. Like maybe he already is.

It's wrong and I hate it and it is not Logan's fault and it makes me all kinds of angry at the world and the universe every atom in it.

But if I can keep my mind on these pages I don't have to care. I can make this all just go away. Poof. I can stay in this book and then this book gets to be real and everything else gets to be fake and who cares anyway.

But no such luck because of all the gin joints in all the world Becky Vilhauer just walked into this one. With Shelli in tow.

She is not happy. Shelli stands behind her looking like she wishes she could hide in her elbow.

"What the fuck?! Seriously?"

"Um . . . would you like fries with that?"

"Ha-ha. Very funny. What's this about Logan McDonough? Seriously."

"What do you mean?"

"Don't play dumb. I know all about it."

"All about what?"

"How about the moped rides . . . after school . . . ring a bell . . . ?"

Becky's leaning in like a vulture. Shelli's getting smaller and smaller with each sentence. The only thing to do is shrug it off.

"It was cold."

"Tsh. Not that cold. Lemme spell it out for you. You're a half-breed. Without me, you're nothing. You're no one. You're like a misfit. A leper."

I catch Shelli peeking out from behind Becky, in pain.

"Don't look at her. You think she's gonna stand by you? Who do you think told me?!"

Shelli is literally shaking now. A broken animal. I catch

her eye and she looks down at the ground. Guilty.

"Look, Becky, it's really no big—"

"Oh, it is a big deal. It's a huge deal. You're jeopardizing all of us. Do you think I wanna get a rep for hanging out with losers? No thanks."

"He's really not that—"

"Get it straight. Either drop him. Or we drop you. And then, I can't be responsible for *whatever happens*."

"That's so—"

"End of story."

And now she turns, Shelli practically attached to her by a leash. Shelli scurries out, ahead of her somehow. Becky turns. A final say.

"Look, this is up to you, Anika. The choice is yours."

And with that she goes out the glass door, into the freezing air. The skeleton decorations smile up at me but I can't return the favor. So much for an uneventful evening.

thirty-eight

I should've known Shelli'd come by at noon. It's Saturday and Shelli is out on the front porch, her cheeks red in the freezing cold. With those red cheeks and saucer eyes it's like Frosty the Snowman is waiting out there for me. My mom lets her in and we go down to the rec room. We've got a pool table down here, a fake bar where the ogre serves root beer (woo hoo!), and a dartboard I can't hit if my life depended on it. Normally, Shelli and I would go to my room and giggle all over the place but it feels too close. Considering she just betrayed me, she gets the rec room.

"Are you mad?"

Shrug. Of course I'm mad. What am I, Jesus?

"I'm really sorry."

"I know."

"She just, like, got it out of me. I mean, she just kept asking questions and then questions and questions and pretty soon it just didn't add up and she kept on me and I caved. I just caved. I'm really sorry. I suck. I know. I totally blew it."

Silence.

The fact is . . . that's how Becky operates.

"Yeah, I can see it."

"You can?"

"Yeah. I mean. I can picture it."

"It really was like I didn't know what was happening and then it just like came out."

"I know."

"Do you forgive me?"

"Well . . . I'm not gonna lie. I was pretty bummed last night. I mean, when you guys left I felt like somebody punched me in the gut or something."

"I know. I'm really sorry. I didn't even know we were going in there till we were there. You know Becky. It was like a sneak attack. Wait, I know!"

Shelli is suddenly excited. She has an idea. This is rare.

"I know how to make it up to you. I'll tell you something I'm not supposed to tell you. No matter what."

"Yeah?"

"Yeah."

"Okay."

"Okay, so you know that whole Stacy Nolan thing? The pregnancy scare?"

"Yeah?"

"That was Becky."

"What?"

"Becky started that."

"What? No way."

"Way."

"But . . . why?"

"For fun."

"Are you serious?"

"Totally. Stacy did nothing to Becky. Becky was just . . . bored."

"What a bitch!"

"I know."

"That's like so mean."

"I. Know."

Shelli and I look at each other with disbelief in our eyes and there's something else in there, too . . . fear. If Becky could do something like that, on a whim, just think what she could do to us.

It's terrifying. Now I know why Shelli caved. She knew, even more than me, the true nature of the beast. I would've caved, too, to be honest.

"Anyway, do you forgive me? . . . Please? You're like my best friend."

"Yeah. I do. I mean, I was mad but I get it. I do."

Awkward hug. I've never been very good at hugs. I'd honestly just rather shake hands. The less humanoid contact the better. But Shelli means it. I can tell. She's never been much of a liar. I make a note to myself. Don't tell Shelli anything. Not because I'm mad. Just because she's defenseless against Becky. Becky will get it out of her. No matter what.

Shelli is down the steps and putting on her coat. She turns to me.

"What are you doing tonight?"

Tonight, meaning Saturday night. Meaning my date with Jared. Meaning the Oscars and the Super Bowl and the Second Coming all in one.

"Oh, nothing."

Shelli nods, unconvinced. Normally, she'd ask me to hang out but it's kinda premature considering we just made up. Might be awkward. I don't hold it against her, though. Shelli's a good egg. She's just not very strong-willed. Her weird Christian mom snuffed any will out of her.

"Call me."

"Yeah. Tomorrow."

And with that, Shelli is gone. Just in time for me to start planning my outfit.

I know what you're thinking. What's wrong with me? And I would be thinking the same thing about you if our roles were reversed. I would. But the point is, it's clear that ever since Jared came to my door, I've been possessed by voodoo witch doctors who have obviously cast a spell on me to make me unable to stop myself from going out on this date with Jared. It's not my fault. Their power is too strong.

thirty-nine

Nobody knows about my date with Jared Kline. Except my sisters, who are pissed. My brothers probably forgot by now. Robby doesn't care because the Knights lost to the Spartans last night, so he's been moping around all day.

The thing is, after tonight, *everyone* will know about my date with Jared Kline. Because at least two or three people will be at this Halloween jamboree thingy and that means by midnight the whole school will know. And by the whole school, I mean everyone. And by everyone, I mean Logan. Logan will find out by Monday for sure. I think.

I don't know how to feel about this other than the way I feel, which is decidedly . . . okay, look, I don't know how I feel about it, okay? Jesus.

But the thing is . . . Let's say I do go out on the date, and let's say I don't like Jared Kline at all. Then I can just tell Logan . . . um . . . I don't know what I can tell Logan. I'm not sure IF I can tell him anything without thinking about him pummeling that guy's brains out by the boathouse.

But I'll think of something. I will. Maybe I could just tell him that I wasn't really that romanced by the fact that he almost killed someone in front of me. Or maybe I can tell him I'm in love with him and think he's kind of a hero and maybe we should run off together and become some sort of Bonnie-and-Clyde bank-robber duo.

As you can see, folks, I haven't thought this thing through. And how can I? There's really no playbook for what to do when you're sort of in love with an unstable misfit and then the biggest heartthrob in history asks you out on a date, an official date where he asks your parents and everything.

I mean, not going on the date? That's like, well, I mean, that's like not going to the moon or something. Like Neil Armstrong just shrugging and saying, yeah, I'll pass.

And yes, there is the distinct possibility he might just be the world's greatest scam artist. That's true. But how am I gonna know if I don't even go on one date? It's just one date. That's it. One date. No big deal.

Also, don't forget the voodoo possession.

The tricky thing about getting dressed up and going

anywhere in Lincoln, Nebraska, from October to March is that it's freezing, goddammit, so what are you supposed to wear? It's like a balancing act where you're trying to find the happy medium between Marilyn Monroe and the Stay Puft Marshmallow Man. I mean, you need a coat. And boots. And you basically have to wear three layers everywhere. So, go ahead, you try to make that look sexy.

The best I can do is two pairs of tights, boots, a parka, a hat, and . . . a miniskirt. That's the sexy part. Look, I'm doing my best. The fact is, dressing for an indoor/outdoor Halloween jamboree is a fashion dilemma of the order Jean Paul Gaultier couldn't solve. I get an A for effort.

My mom is waiting with me, fixing dinner, while I pretend to not be nervous at the table. She's got the ceramic Halloween salt and pepper shakers on the table. Oh, you didn't know? My mom has ceramic salt and pepper shakers, table decorations, even china for every holiday from here till Christmas. This is the heavy decorating time of the year. She has boxes for Halloween. For Thanksgiving. Five for Christmas. We take the holidays seriously here. We're not fooling around.

The ceramic Halloween salt and pepper shakers are an undead couple. It's really very appetizing to eat your dinner staring at bleeding, drooling statues of his-and-hers brain-eaters. My mom can tell I'm nervous.

"It's alright, honey. He's just a boy. Besides, he's the one who asked you out."

"I know, Mom."

"And if anything makes you feel uncomfortable, I want you to come straight home. You can call anytime. I'll be here by the phone."

"Thanks, Mom."

"Or you can even take a cab. I'll give you cab fare. Just in case."

"Okay, Mom."

"Just be yourself."

"Mom, I'm nervous."

"I know, honey. But don't be. Just try to have fun, okay? Try to live in the moment."

"Mom, are you a hippie?"

She smiles. No one else in the family jokes around with my mom like this, I don't know why. She always gets the joke. I guess everybody's just too wrapped up in their own drama to notice. But I know it means a lot to her. To know I see her. To know I love her. I swear to God without her I'd be one of the first female serial killers in history.

"Listen, this boy is lucky to be spending time with you. Think of it like that."

"Tsh. Yeah, right."

"He is! Believe you me."

The doorbell rings now and my heart jumps out of my chest onto the table. Jesus. This is terrible. This is going to be the worst night ever. I better not even talk. I'll just smile and nod. And laugh. But not too much. And not too loud. Just a nice laugh. Supportive. Jesus. What is wrong with me? I'm falling apart.

This is gonna be a total disaster.

My mom opens the door and there is Jared. He's wearing a navy blue North Face parka, jeans, and hiking boots. Pure Jared.

Even though I can't see it, I can tell you right now that underneath that parka somewhere he's wearing a Led Zeppelin T-shirt. The one where the angel is falling from the sky.

He smiles up at me and it kinda sorta maybe knocks the wind out of me. Oh my God. This is gonna be excruciating. Maybe I should just say I'm sick and crawl into my bed. I could just pretend I came down with something and run away.

"Hello, ma'am. I've come for that aforementioned date with your daughter."

"Yes, come on in. There's no reason to stand out in the cold."

Jared comes in and I can see my sisters peeking in from down the hall. I catch Lizzie's eye and she mouths, "You are SO dead."

Jared is standing there waiting for me, next to my mom.

This is my last chance to bail. I really could just say I'm not feeling well.

"Honey, are you ready?"

My mom is trying to make everything normal. Poor Mom. She has no idea she's raised a neurotic Muppet who's falling apart.

"Anika? You ready?"

That's Jared. Gulp. I realize I've never been on an actual date before.

"This is my first date!" I blurt.

Wow. What a nerd. I bet he just walks off now.

"That's awesome! I must be the luckiest guy in the universe then."

He smiles. My mom smiles. Everyone's just smiling their faces off.

Okay, here goes nothing.

I step forward and before I know it Jared and I are out the door. Out out out into the brisk night air where you can see your breath and your eyeballs are freezing and you can get in a dark green Jeep and go to the Halloween jamboree thingy where everyone in town is gonna see you're on a date with THE Jared Kline.

forty

All the little kids at the Halloween Spookfest are dressed up like ghouls and goblins, warlocks and witches. It's like a miniature underworld. There are also a lot of mini Luke Skywalkers, Han Solos, and Darth Vaders. Even some mini Stormtroopers. And a mini Chewbacca. That's the one everyone's going gaga over. The kid's like four. And he's got that Wookiee call down cold.

There's a haunted house, a pumpkin patch, a fortune-teller, and bobbing for apples.

So far we've had hot cider and doughnuts and Jared has tried (and failed) to win me a black-and-orange cat doll in the Ping-Pong toss game. He is strolling around the festival like he's the mayor of Halloween.

Head held high, it's like he's nine feet tall or something.

"Can I ask you a question?" I can't help myself.

"Shoot."

"Why are you so happy all the time?"

"Why shouldn't I be? It's a beautiful night, the moon is out, that kid's dressed like Chewbacca, and I'm with the most beautiful girl in the world."

"Um. I think you mean you're with the most beautiful girl in this pumpkin patch."

"Well, this pumpkin patch is the world right now. Feels like it anyway."

I would gag if this were uttered by any other being on the planet.

We walk around a group of mini-princesses in pink and purple, waving their magic wands.

"For a scam artist, you're really convincing. I'd say you're excellent."

"Thank you but I'm not a scam artist. Anika, seriously, I'm not. People just say that because they're jealous or stupid or they're just looking for something to talk about."

I don't know what to say to that. I think of that Stacy Nolan debacle. That was a complete fantasy. And everyone gobbled it up like candy corn.

Two stands down, Jenny Schnittgrund is sipping an apple cider with Charlie Russell.

We walk by and they both proceed to spill cider all over the place, faces agog. And they're off! Let the rumor mill churn!

Now Jared stops abruptly and turns to me.

"There's just something about you, Anika. You're . . . mysterious or something."

"Mysterious. Like the part where I blurted out I've never been on a date before?"

"Yeah, that part." He smirks. "No, but seriously. I don't know, I just kind of, like, think about you. Like a lot."

"Really?"

"Yeah."

"Why?"

"Man, you really aren't vain, I'll give you that."

The pumpkin patch is getting a little crazy with miniature goblins so we head to the haunted house, presumably so Jared can try to ravish me in the dark. You have to buy the tickets first so I wait in line while Jared goes to the ticket booth.

Mostly I'm just standing there wondering if this is some joke like in that movie where the girl gets blood spilled all over her at prom. I mean. Jared Kline. *The* Jared Kline, acting like this. It's like a parallel universe I've stepped into.

Right now there are two miniature Ewoks trying to convince the haunted house guy he should let them in. He keeps telling them they're too little and they keep giving him examples of things they've been able to do, even though they're too little. Like see *Superman*. And drive a go-cart. Even the haunted house guy is getting a kick out of it. We smile at each other. Yeah, they're cute, you can't deny it.

The Ewoks continue to make their case. At that moment all of this sweetness and light and goodwill to all mankind is ruined by the scariest creature of all at the Halloween Spookfest:

Becky Vilhauer.

I shoulda known.

She's standing there like she's been there for hours and Shelli's behind her, again, looking like a lost kitten. They're dressed up, too. Like bitches. I mean, witches.

"You. Are. So. Busted."

"Um. Hi."

"Thought you could come promenade around with your super-nerd, huh?"

"What?"

"I can't believe how stupid you are. Did you really think you could just walk around with that total nerd-face and we wouldn't find out? I mean, it's like, you're like brain-dead or something—"

"Evening, ladies."

Jared is back. He's got the tickets.

If you could peel the expression off someone's face like the label on a jar, I would want these two expressions to go on my wall for the rest of my life.

Becky looks like aliens just landed. Shelli looks like Jesus just levitated.

I mean, never in the history of time have two girls been sucker punched thusly.

God, I wish my eye were a camera.

Becky tries to pull it together.

"I-I just. Hey, Jared."

"Hey," Shelli squeaks.

But now, Becky won't be satisfied. She must have her day. She must win.

"What are you doing here with him? I thought you had a *boyfriend?*"

And there it is. My night of a thousand wonders comes to an end. No more sweet words in the pumpkin patch. He'll probably just leave me here. Becky would just love that. She'll make me beg for a ride home. Seriously. Oh well. I guess I'll just call my mom.

Except that Jared says this:

"She does have a boyfriend."

And then he picks me up like he's carrying me over the threshold or something and looks Becky straight in the eye.

"Me."

And with that, he swoops me off into the night of a thousand goblins and lets the tickets fall to the ground because who cares about that Halloween house ride when you've got Jared Kline carrying you and you might as well be on a rocket ship.

forty-one

We're in Jared's Jeep now, speeding home. He turns to me.

"Sorry we didn't get to go on that ride or whatever. But I think we both know what was the scariest thing at the Halloween Spookfest."

"Hm?"

"Beeeeecky Viiilhaaaauuuueeer." He makes his hands into claws and pretends to claw me.

I really never would've thought Jared Kline would be this witty. I thought he was just like maybe of average intelligence, kind of a burnout at best. I mean, his kid brother, Brad, once raised his hand in biology and asked if trees were alive. That's a true story, by the way.

"So, what are we doing now?"

"Well, since I'm such a total scam artist, I'm taking you home now so your mom doesn't freak."

"Touché."

"Oh, so you speak French?"

"*Je ne parle pas français.* That means I don't speak French."

"Ooh la la. Who taught you that?"

"My brother. Henry. Sometimes we nerd out together. He loves everything French."

"I see . . . French toast, French dressing, French fries . . ."

" . . . French's mustard."

Jared smiles at me and now we're just total goofballs. But I'm terrified when we get to my house. I'm dying when we get to my house. My heart is leaping out of my sweater when we get to my house. What will he do? Will he kiss me? Do I want him to kiss me? Yes, I want him to kiss me. No, I don't want him to kiss me. What if I'm not a very good kisser? Why should I be? The only person I've ever kissed before is my not-not-not boyfriend Logan.

We pull up to the driveway and he turns off the engine. I guess he thinks this is make-out city.

"Here, I'll walk you to your door."

"Oh, you don't have to—"

"C'mon, you never know what kind of skeletons might be waiting in the bushes. You saw those kids. They're out for blood."

I hop out of the Jeep and head for the door. Most of the lights are off in the front of the house, so I guess no one can see us. Maybe. You never know.

"So, um, Anika. You made my night kinda."

"Really?"

"Yeah, you did. I like being with you, standing next to you."

"Wow. I don't know what to—"

"That thing I said about you being my girlfriend? Anika, I want you to be."

"But this is crazy. You don't even know me! Don't you have like a million—"

"No. I don't." He sighs. "Look, I don't know what you've heard about me or where you heard it or whatever but I'm not *bad*. I'm just a guy. You know? All that stuff you hear is just . . . noise."

"Okay."

"So, you're my girlfriend now?"

"I guess?"

Every time I talk it sounds like I'm speaking from under a rock. I just can't believe any of it and I feel like if I talk too loud I'll break it. I'll wake up and realize it was all just a dream.

I touch the gold necklace hanging from my neck.

"I'm not gonna kiss you, Anika."

"What? Why not?" That sounded bad. "I mean—"

"Because I know there's a part of you that still thinks I'm a scam artist. And I wanna prove to you I'm not. I'm just a guy. Who likes you."

A light goes on in the living room up above us.

"I guess that's my mom."

"Good night, Anika." He squeezes me on the shoulder, reassuringly.

Okay, no one's ever squeezed me on the shoulder reassuringly before.

And then he goes, back to his Jeep, back into whatever cloud in the sky he came from. He turns before getting in.

"Sweet dreams."

And then he's off, and there I am standing on the front porch, wondering what just happened. And he's right. I will have sweet dreams because this was all a sweet dream and I feel like I'm the girl whose sweet dreams never come true and I wonder how long this sweet dream can possibly last.

forty-two

Pedaling fast fast fast, the back wheel, rusty, goes squeak squeak squeak. This is the moment, this is the moment and now the trees and the leaves and the sidewalk give way and now there's blue and red circles and sirens and red-and-white trucks and the trees and the leaves and the sidewalk whisper they tried to stop me they tried to stop me they did.

Pedaling fast fast fast, don't see it. Try not to see it, don't see it but there is no way not to see it, there is no way to go back now.

Pedaling fast fast fast, this is the moment. You thought you could change it, remember how you thought you could change it and you want to laugh out loud you thought that but there is no laughing, there is no laughing now.

forty-three

I know what to do now about Tiffany. I've been racking my brain since the night she got fired and now I know the only way to make it better. Or even get close to making it better. I have to give her the money. I bet you're wondering how much it is. How much did little miss front clerk and her sidekick Shelli steal from the Bunza-a-meal-in-a-Bunza?

Answer:

(Drumroll, please . . .)

Exactly one thousand two hundred thirty-six dollars and fifty cents. Yes, ladies and gentlemen. That looks like this: $1,236.50.

And Tiffany is gonna get all of it.

Don't try to talk me out of it, I've already decided. I'm

halfway over to her house and my nose has already frozen off my face, thank you very much. This is one of those crappy almost-winter days where the sky is the color of oatmeal and the ground is frozen white, not even any snow to give it character. Just cold and suicide-inducing.

My dad, the vampire, likes to say, "Dees veather. Eet punishes you." And he's right. You do get the feeling you're getting punished for something. But what? Maybe punished for living in such a crappy place and not doing anything about it, that's what.

Let's talk depressing. This stucco apartment building might as well have a sign out front reading "WE KIND OF BLEW IT." I mean, anybody who isn't in college or going through a horrible divorce has got to be feeling pretty lame calling this place home. It doesn't help that there's a Burger King right across the street. I mean, the whole place smells like cheeseburgers.

When I get to the door I decide this is a stupid idea anyway and I'm leaving. What if she's not home and her mean mom answers? I can't give *her* the money. She'll probably just spend it on stuff to make her meaner. Whatever that is. I guess I'd be grumpy, too, if I had to live in this shit-basket.

The door opens before I even knock and it's Tiffany. She stands there looking at me, and it's like she's shrinking somehow right before my eyes.

"Hey."

I know. I have a way with words.

"Hey." Still shrinking.

"Listen, um . . . Hey, can I come in? It's kinda cold. . . ."

"Um, really?"

Oh. I get it. Tiffany doesn't want me to see this place. That I understand. I didn't really want Jared to see my place either. Not after seeing that library with nautical oil paintings.

"Yeah, I mean. It's kinda like freezing out here."

"Okay."

I step in and it's not all that bad, actually. I mean, it's not like you could eat off the floor, like our house. The corners are grimy. But there's an effort at sweeping and dusting that ends up somewhere between yeah-that's-enough and who-cares-anyway.

So far, no sign of Mom. Thank God.

"So, I felt kinda bad that, um, you got busted, so—"

"I know. It was stupid. I dunno what—"

"No, you don't have to say you're sorry."

"No, I am—"

Oh my God, am I gonna tell her? She could so bust me if I do. And Shelli. Mr. Baum would press charges, too. $1,236.50 worth of charges. Probably more for his wounded pride. And the fact he's short. And fat. And that

I've been poisoning him.

"Look, Tiffany, we stole, too."

"What?"

Oh Lord. Tiffany looks like I just told her aliens landed in Topeka. This is gonna suck. Please God, don't let her tell on me.

"Yeah, we did. I had a whole system—"

"But why?"

"'Cause I'm an idiot."

"But you're rich."

"I guess, not rich enough?"

She and I just stand there looking at each other. Maybe it dawns on both of us that you can never be rich enough. Maybe that's the problem.

"Look, we were idiots."

"Shelli, too?"

"Yeah."

"But her mom's a Christian."

"Exactly."

Tiffany smiles.

"Look, there's just no reason why. I'm kind of a shitty person, I guess that's why."

"No, you're not. You saved my ass!"

"Well, maybe, but mostly just 'cause I felt guilty. Anyway . . . here."

I hand Tiffany the money, wrapped up in a Bunza Hut wrapper. She looks inside and then looks closer and closer and her eyes are practically popping out. Right into that Bunza Hut wrapper, where we could serve them up with fries.

"Holy shit!"

"I know. It's a lot."

"How did you—"

I shrug. "We had a system."

Tiffany looks at me. I can tell her opinion of me is changing rapidly by the millisecond.

"I thought you were perfect."

"Um . . . no."

"Well, you're pretty clever. Maybe that's it."

"Thanks. When I was little they thought I was retarded and then they tested me and I had like a high IQ so I'm kind of like a smart retard."

"How much is here?"

"Like about . . . one thousand two hundred thirty-six dollars and fifty cents. But who's counting?"

Tiffany looks around. God, I hope her mother's not home.

"I can't take this."

"Yes, you can. And you will. You have to. I can't live with myself if you don't. I really can't."

"Are you sure?"

"Yup."

"Well, what am I supposed to do with it?"

"Don't give it to your mom. That's for sure."

"No shit."

She and I have a moment of silence. What do you do with money? Everybody's so crazy about it but then, once you get it, what do you do with it? Hug it?

"Maybe put it in the bank or something?"

"Yeah. That's a good idea. Thanks. Thank you so much."

"No. Don't. I'm a jerk. Don't thank me."

"Did you give this to me because you feel sorry for me?"

"I don't think so."

"Good."

We hear someone's feet on the stairs outside and both of us freeze in fear. Please don't let it be her mom. Please don't let it be her mom.

"Okay, I better go. Call me, or come by, whenever. I'm around."

"Yeah, I will. I'll call you."

And I know when I'm shuffling down those stairs, past the stucco and wrought-iron gates, I know she'll never call. I know she'll never call and never come by—ever again.

forty-four

So far today the sun is playing a trick where it's shining so bright it looks like it's supposed to be seventy degrees but then you go outside and it's thirty.

It's almost the end of the week. Thursday. The best day. All the anticipation of the weekend but none of the dread.

I've pretty much been skipping out on everybody, including Shelli, taking different routes to class. . . . I dunno. I just don't really seem to know what to do about anything anymore so I'm hiding. If I could turn this ceiling into a blanket and crawl under it, I would.

We're on seventies installations in Stoner Art Teacher's class and, so far, all I've got is a bright white diorama shoe box and no clue what to do with it.

I guess the general idea is you're just supposed to create a space where everybody walks in and has an emotional reaction.

I resolve to make a space where everybody walks in and is terrified.

Mostly right now my brilliant idea is sitting somewhere inside my head, hiding from me, and the only way to get it out seems to be to sit here and stare out the window.

Praise Jesus! The alarm bell goes off and once again we are all shuffled off outside, into the freezing cold, and everyone is looking at me expectantly.

"What? I didn't do it!"

Just like last time we wait, stare at each other, make chit-chat, watch our breath come out in dragon puffs, and go back inside, finally, before we are all taken to the hospital for hypothermia.

I guess I won't have to work too hard to think of an installation because once we get back inside, there's . . . um . . . an installation.

This is what it is:

The entire room is filled with, teeming with . . . butterflies.

And not just any old butterflies . . . but the most beautiful butterflies you've ever seen.

Bright blue butterflies, almost purple in the light, flying

all over the place, catching the bright blue light in their wings. Hundreds of them.

Just so you know, I've heard of this before. My mom said my aunt did this at her wedding out in Berkeley, where everybody's a socialist but kind of a hippie but kind of rich, too, and interested in butterfly extravaganzas, I guess. She said they released these butterfly packets after the ceremony and everybody sighed and whistled but then all the butterflies immediately died and it was really awkward and sort of depressing. But these butterflies aren't dying. In fact, they seem to be thriving in this artistic environment.

Now, of course, everyone is freaking out. There are *oohs* and *aahs*, and *dudes* and *no ways*, and the heshers are tripping out. Some of the girls are actually scared of the butterflies or something. Or maybe they're just pretending to get attention. Yup. That's exactly what they're doing. I mean, since when are butterflies scary?

If you were going to make a movie about a rabid butterfly, everyone would just laugh in your face. Although, I guess this imaginary scenario would take place in Hollywood so who knows what would happen? Maybe they would just laugh in your face and do a line of coke off the nearest starlet.

Note to self. Never go to Hollywood.

PS: Everyone is looking at me.

I guess this qualifies as a successful installation.

My white shoe box diorama is still at my workstation and there's no amazing painting there to replace it or anything so I am officially off the hook for this.

But that doesn't mean that this isn't 100 percent, completely, a zillion percent, the work of Logan McDonough. If there was any doubt, I notice there's a little fake blue butterfly pinned to the side of my Trapper Keeper. I know this because there has never before been a little fake blue butterfly pinned to the side of my Trapper Keeper.

And if you think this makes me fall totally, completely in love with Logan, well, you are wrong. I refuse to do it, no matter what, so just stop it.

Also, if you think that I have been sitting around missing Logan and wishing that I'd turn the corner and see him hiding in the bushes and then he'd just come up and grab me and knock my socks off with a kiss that erases everything that happened and this weird Jared voodoo spell would be lifted, well, that's not true either. I swear.

Stoner Art Teacher turns to me.

"Anika? Was this your project?"

I know, I know. I am supposed to be a good person and always say please and thank-you and never say anything mean and always tell the truth.

I pause and then—

"Do I get an A?"

forty-five

Bet you're wondering what I'm gonna do about Logan now, huh? Well, you're not the only one. Seriously this is not how I thought this was gonna play out. Like AT ALL. How was I supposed to know that out of nowhere this seeming Prince Charming in a Led Zeppelin T-shirt who everybody worships was gonna come at me with all guns blazing?

It doesn't help that everybody thinks Jared is a super-god and Logan is a super-dork, even though he's kind of like an artistic genius maybe. I know, I know. I shouldn't care about the dork part. Why should I? But the truth is . . . I do. Like, I really do. Let's just call it like it is, no need to pretty it up. I care what other people think of me. I'm not Jesus Christ. I'm just a girl in the world.

Also, I won't even speak about . . .

You know, that guy at the boathouse was a whiskey-breath scuz-bucket who was probably going to kidnap me and bury me alive in his trailer park.

And Logan has set off not one but two, count 'em, two, fire alarms to impress me. Although, to be quite honest, I'm not sure if that fake fire alarm thing puts him in the crazy column or the genius column. Jury's out. I mean, listen, the whole thing just swirls around and around in my head and never lands.

It's maddening.

All of this is why I went to bed early tonight, locked myself inside my room, so I could just stare at the ceiling and ask God what in the world to do. I know a lot of people think that whole God thing is a joke but I just get a feeling he's up there somewhere. There're too many things for him not to be. Like, for instance, everything. Like, where did it all come from? Of course there was a big bang, no shit. But what was before that? Who made the big bang in the first place? Anybody ever wonder about that part? Look. He's there and I just know it. Anybody who thinks we are the most intelligent life in the universe has obviously never been to Nebraska.

Trust me.

My mom got me this night-light thingy that projects the cow jumping over the moon, spinning around in little circles above me on the ceiling. Happy, smiling stars surround the moon and it plays a little lullaby, which I turned down, but I did realize, at some point, this is a night-light for babies. I guess my mom thinks I need a lot of coddling. Maybe she's right. If I don't have the night-light I can't get to sleep. Like ever. It's like a curse if I don't have it and it's a sign of certain doom. We left it once when we went to visit my aunt and my mom had to drive back and get it because I couldn't sleep for like two days. Again, this is the part where everybody in the family refers to me as "special." It's not a compliment. It means there's a screw loose.

So right now I'm just staring at the cow jumping over the moon and wondering what I'm gonna say to Logan. I was thinking I could say something like this:

"Logan. I'm an idiot. I don't know what to do but you should probably stay away from me because I'm confused and have no self-esteem and, also, I think you might be a sociopath. But look, you are amazing and cool and sometimes I think about shrinking myself down and fitting myself into your pocket so I can live there forever, but, then, I worry that maybe you are not exactly playing with a full deck and you might turn on me and take me out of your pocket and squash me like a bug next to the boathouse."

That's what I've got so far.

I also was thinking I could try to say it with flowers.

That thought, which makes no sense, is running through my head when there's a thud on my window, right above my head. Then another thud. Then another. If the ogre hears that, I'm gonna get it, so I look out the window and there he is, through the trees from below. Logan. Standing under my window like some mod Romeo.

Guess I won't be saying it with flowers.

The window creaks when I open it. Not good. This whole thing could lead to at least a two-week grounding if the ogre wakes up.

"Logan! Shh! What the—"

"Okay, I know you're mad at me. I get it . . . but I wanna show you something—"

"I can't. Are you kidding?!"

We're both whisper-screaming at each other. All I can think is this is the worst possible way to break up with somebody.

"C'mon. Please? It's supercool. Seriously."

"No, I can't. I can't risk it. Lemme call you tomorrow—"

"Pretty please?"

"No."

"No? Anika, c'mon. Seriously."

Ugh. I'm really gonna have to do this, aren't I? Like right now, in the middle of the night through a freezing-cold window.

"Logan, just lemme call you later, when—"

And now there's a moment when something in the air changes. All the puppy love turns prickly and Logan straightens up.

"What the fuck, Anika?"

"What?"

But, of course, I know what he means. I'm blowing him off. I'm blowing him off because he did that psycho thing and even though he did all that other cool stuff it doesn't matter now 'cause Jared Kline has swept me off my feet and even though I feel bad and feel like I've led him on and we did have all that romance and fake fire alarms and sneaky moped rides, even though it felt, for a little while, like we were in our own private movie, now all that is changed, all that is changed and he didn't know it and now he knows it and he's fucking bummed.

And he's looking up at me like a sinking ship.

"Logan, it's just. I just . . . well, I think we should slow down or something."

Slow down? You mean stop. You mean stop and he knows it and you know it and he'll really know it any day now 'cause practically everybody knows that you're Jared Kline's girlfriend.

"What? What do you . . . what the fuck, Anika?!"

"Logan—"

"What? The boathouse? Is that it? Look, I told you, I lost it! But I was protecting *you*."

"I know, it's just. I don't know what to say. I—"

"'Kay, I'll say it. How 'bout I say it for you? You're a coward, how 'bout that? You're a fucking coward who can't stand up to your dumb friends."

And he's right. In a way. He is.

"No, it's just—"

"Anika. I get it. Alright? I fucking get it."

He starts to walk away.

Now the cold air is sweeping in and I can't tell if it's the cold air or me that's making my eyes water. Must be the air. I can't care about this. I can't.

He turns around.

"Just so you know. I fucking loved you. I fucking loved the daylights out of you."

And now the tears slide down and he's off, through the trees and down the sidewalk. And now I'm sitting there, closing the window and staring into my reflection and I don't mind telling you, ladies and gentlemen, I don't like what I see.

forty-six

The next day something happens that I'd like to call The Greatest Moment Ever Told. Keep in mind that my whole life I've kinda like been a second-class citizen in this place. You know, it's always been like a feeling of "don't get too ahead of yourself" or "know your place."

You're not one of us. That's really what it's always been underneath. So, this day, this day here, is basically a moment I never thought was reserved for a girl like me. This is a moment for Becky or Shelli, or someone else with a normal last name. Not a freak with a vampire dad and a name you have to say three times before anybody gets it.

The sun decided to make a comeback after school so this is one of those fall crisp days where the sky is the color of a bright blue marble and you can walk outside without seeing your breath. Becky and Shelli are walking ahead and I'm behind Shelli like a poodle but there's something up ahead and I know it's big because when we walk out, there might as well be a record scratch. It's like crickets out here, not a sound, even though there's a zillion people and even though they are seeming to part like the Red Sea, leaving Becky, Shelli, and me in the middle like Moses. Except now Becky and Shelli step aside and it's just me. Now I'm Moses. And Shelli whispers something—I think she's whispering to me but I can't hear it. And Becky whispers something, and I think that's for me, too, but I can't hear. I can't hear because all I can do is see and all I can see is Jared Kline.

He's standing there, leaning against his Jeep like Elvis.

And he's looking at me.

He smiles when he sees me, like the cat that ate the canary and then ate all the canary's little brothers and sisters and the canary's grandma, too. He's smiling the only way you get to smile if you've got every single person in the town, county, state in love with you.

And everyone, everyone you've ever even thought about, is out here to witness. Jenny Schnittgrund. Chip Rider. Stacy Nolan. Joel Soren. Charlie Russell. The whole ensemble.

But you should see Becky. It's like she's having an allergic reaction. It's like she's about to break out in hives. She can't believe it. Right in front of her face, it's happening. But she can't believe it's happening and doesn't want to believe it's happening and is terrified because she knows it is. But there's something else in it, too, a calculation.

And as Jared Kline comes up the steps, yes, folks, comes up the steps to meet me, and kiss me on the cheek, in front of everybody, and grab my books out of my hands, in front of everybody, Becky leans in and gives me a whisper.

"We should hang out more."

Seriously, that's the best she's got. Just an obvious, unabashed change of tune. No more "half-breed," no more "immigrant." Just a desperate, pathetic, shameless attempt. We should hang out more.

Yes, Becky. We should hang out more. You should hang out with a half-breed immigrant like me and tell me what to do more.

And then there is Shelli. I don't even have to look at her but I can feel it. She's like a proud parent or something. She's practically leaping out of her dress.

But now there is no such thing as Becky and Shelli. Now there is only Jared Kline. Now there is only walking down the steps with Jared Kline carrying my books. Now there is only Jared Kline opening the passenger side and making a gesture like he's some knight or something. Now there is only Jared Kline hopping in the driver's side and gunning the engine and driving off like we might as well be flying into space.

And what about the rearview? In the rearview the entirety of Pound High School is a student body of open mouths, and front and center, jaw dropped, is Becky Vilhauer.

forty-seven

Most people don't know this but all you have to do is drive due east from Lincoln and you get into the area, out in the sticks, where it's all rolling hills and mud and dirt roads with a farmhouse every once in a while. It's the kind of place where you better not get lost, or lose a tire, because that means a lot of walking for you and maybe getting picked up by a serial killer who will put you in the basement and try to eat your kidneys.

Driving up and down these rolling hills with Jared Kline you could almost get dizzy. It's just up up up and down down down and up again. It's like being on a roller coaster made of dirt and starting to freeze over.

Jared stops the Jeep in no particular place. Like, he

254

literally stops the Jeep in the middle of the hill. Now, there's not a car around for miles, I get it. But still. He doesn't even pull off the side of the road or anything. So, why are we stopped here? None of this bodes well.

"Um. Maybe we shouldn't stop in the middle of the road or something."

I hear my voice and it sounds like it's made of tin. Not my voice at all. Someone else's voice. Someone small.

"Oh, c'mon. There's no one around."

"But . . . I mean . . . I thought you were gonna show me someplace special?"

Jared nods. He gestures out the window, at the rolling hills and panoramic postcard view.

"You don't think this is special?"

"I guess."

"Oh, c'mon, what's the matter? Is something the matter . . . ?"

There are about a hundred things the matter.

"I dunno. There's this girl at work. She got fired."

Why I chose that one is beyond me. It just came flying out and now I guess that's the topic of conversation here in the middle of nowhere.

"Yeah?"

He feigns interest.

"Yeah, I guess I'm bummed 'cause it wasn't fair. Like it

was really mean, actually."

Silence.

"You know what I mean? Like I just felt guilty."

Jared shrugs. "What's the point of feeling guilty?"

"What?"

"I mean, it doesn't seem like it's helping, does it?"

"I dunno."

"Listen, it's not your fault, right? So, forget it."

He shrugs again. God, this guy can really shrug.

But he's quiet and bored and seems like a stranger all of a sudden. Like, what happened to that grandiose-type gesture he just made in front of everybody at school? This makes no sense. *He* makes no sense. It's like he switched gears in like two seconds. Without warning. Like he turned from Prince Charming into a wet noodle.

"You know, I probably should get going home. My mom'll be worried about me."

"C'mon. You can stay out a little while. . . ."

And now he's getting closer. He's giving me this smolder-y look like we're in some kind of soap opera.

Aha! This is the Jared everybody told me about! The make-out bandit. The scam artist that I knew I shouldn't trust. Here he is, ladies and gentlemen, in all his scam artist glory.

"Wait—" I start. But Jared Kline practically jumps me and

smothers me with his mouth on my mouth. And his hands are someplace, too, and they seem to be trying to go someplace else, fast.

I shove him away. "What the fuck?!"

Now he backs off. Now he's back in his seat.

"Anika?" He blinks a couple of times. "What is the problem?"

"What is the problem? I'm trying to talk to you and it's like you don't care and all you're trying to do is kiss me!"

"Okay, I do care. But also—yes, sue me, I know it's horrible—but I also, yes, do wanna kiss you. 'Cause, guess what? You're fucking hot."

"Great."

He leans back and folds his arms. "Oh, I know. What an insult."

"Look, to be honest. I'm not interested."

He looks at me like no one in his life has ever talked to him like this before. Ever.

"I'm sorry," I mutter. "I just. I think maybe I'm an idiot or something."

He looks at me for about a thousand years and I'm plotting how I'm gonna get home after he kicks me out of the Jeep and the sun is starting to set, early, autumn time, and none of this is exactly how I had planned it. Not at all.

"Wow. You're really . . . hm. You're really kind of . . . hard on yourself. You know that?"

"What?"

"And you're not an idiot, Anika. Not by far."

I'm pretty sure this means he's gonna start the car and drive me home and game over, right? But that's not what happens. Instead, Jared Kline says,

"Are you a virgin?"

"What?! Shut up! Why are you asking me that?!"

Silence.

"I just thought . . . like, by now . . . just wondering, I guess."

"Well, even if I was it's not like I'm gonna tell *you*. Jesus."

"Okay, listen. I'm sorry. Seriously. I'm sorry about that. I'm just kind of thrown off by you or something. Like, I don't know how to act around you."

"Well, join the club. I don't know how to act around anybody."

He nods. "Clearly."

"So listen, here's the deal. There's a million girls who are in love with you and who if you say jump they'll say how high. But like, I'm not one of those girls.

"So, if that's what you're looking for, I mean . . . go get 'em. Be my guest. Seriously. Have at it."

Now he's quiet. Now he looks me right in the eyes. God,

it's like Mick Jagger in the car looking at you or something. Mostly you could just faint from those eyes. Just swoon over and let someone find you in the ditch.

"I know you're not like all those girls. That's why I like you."

He sits there for a second, squinting down at the steering wheel. I have no idea if he's gonna kick me out, attack me again, or turn into a taco at this point. I mean, this guy seems seriously conflicted.

He smiles over. Not a convincing smile. A fake smile, like when you're a little kid at Christmas and someone gives you socks.

"Let's get you home, okay?"

It's a quiet ride back to Lincoln. Thank God he turns on the radio.

"You like U2?"

"What?"

"Here . . ." He turns up the volume.

All the way home we're listening to "Sunday Bloody Sunday" and the sun is going down fast and Jared is singing along like he just happens to be a rock star.

Who is this guy? What does he want from me? I wonder.

And why, in the passenger seat of Jared's car, can I not stop thinking about Logan? Brooding, brilliant Logan, who always tells the truth. And whose heart I have shattered into a million pieces.

forty-eight

When I get home my mom is acting weird. We're making meat loaf tonight and I'm helping her, but my sisters are helping, too, so my mom can't have the heart-to-heart with me I can tell she wants to have. I can tell my mom has something she wants to say because she's acting real formal. She's acting like a person who's trying to act natural so, basically, totally unnatural.

After my sisters go downstairs, she turns to me.

"Have you heard from Tiffany?"

"What? No. Why?"

She looks into the other room, nervous. You would think she was a member of the French Resistance acting like that.

"What, Mom?"

"Well, honey, I got a phone call today . . . from Tiffany's mom and . . ."

"And what?"

"And she's, well, she's . . . missing."

"What?!"

"She says she hasn't seen her now for over two days—"

"Are you serious?"

"Yeah, honey. I am."

"What the . . . ?"

"I know. It's just . . . she thought maybe you might know something."

"What do you mean?"

"Well, she said that Tiffany had been acting strangely. And that when she asked her what was going on . . . she just smiled and said something about you and the Bunza Hut."

"What?!"

"Yeah. This is what she said. . . . She said Tiffany said, 'Why don't you ask Anika?'"

"But what about the Bunza Hut?"

"I don't know. She just said something about the Bunza Hut and you. You don't have any idea where she is?"

"What?! No! Mom, no. I'm like freaked out."

"I know, honey, me too."

Now the ogre walks by and we both pretend to dress

the salad but we're definitely not dressing the salad because who cares about tomatoes and iceberg lettuce and ranch dressing when Tiffany is missing in action and somehow it's my fault.

forty-nine

Pedaling fast fast fast. Keep going, keep going, never mind your legs numb from pedaling, never mind your lungs hollowed out from breathing. And maybe it is all just a dream. And you can wish and you can pray but the cold on your cheeks and your heart pounding fast say it's not true, that this is real, and praying won't help not now, not now.

fifty

The next morning there's a giant red bouquet on our door-step. It's so enormous it's almost embarrassing. Mom brings it up to the dining room table, taking a look at the card.

"Oh, my, look at this. . . ."

My sisters and brothers all glance up from their eggs and bacon. You have to give it up for my mom. Eggs and bacon, or eggs and French toast, or sausage and waffles. I mean, she's not fooling around when it comes to breakfast. She means business. I wonder if Becky's mom pulls out all the stops for breakfast every day of the week, Monday through Sunday, three hundred and sixty-five days a year? I know Shelli's doesn't. And if she did, she'd probably just make pancakes in the shape of Jesus.

"They're for you, Anika."

And there they are, set on the table in front of everybody. God, this is mortifying.

And then, Lizzie leans in. Just to make sure my cheeks sting and my face turns the shade of a lobster.

"That musta been some blow job."

"Shut up! God! You would know!"

Oh, I could kill my sisters sometimes. It's like they live to torture me.

Henry is the only decent one among them. And Robby. But he's always at football practice.

"Well, aren't you gonna read the card, dear?"

My mom didn't hear Lizzie's smart remark, or Lizzie'd be sent to her room.

It's a little pink envelope with a little pink card. Inside, it says:

> Anika,
>   I'm really sorry I kind of attacked you like a rabid dog.
>   I'm an idiot.
>
>   Jared

Well, it's kinda hard to be mad at him, now, isn't it? Henry's curious. Kind of like Spock.

"Well, what does it say?"

Lizzie chimes in again. "It says, thanks for the hot se—"

"Lizzie, that's enough."

Thank God for my mom. If she weren't around, Lizzie would right now be shoving those roses right up my nose and out my earlobes. I'm not kidding. The thing about Lizzie is . . . she may have this waif look going but she's actually kind of strong. Like she can whip my ass every time. It's annoying. She knows I live in fear. She's banking on it.

Henry's still looking, intrigued.

Now it's my turn. "It says, 'Dear Anika, I'm so sorry your older sisters are such sluts. Maybe if they had boobs they would feel better.'"

Now Lizzie is on me and Neener is egging her on.

"You little—"

"Girls! Girls!"

Robby is just looking on over his Froot Loops and laughing. "Girl fight!"

Now, Lizzie has me pinned to the floor and is about to spit in my mouth.

"Lizzie, if you don't get off your sister right now you are grounded for three months. That's the holidays, too. Just you go ahead and try me."

Mom saves the day again. Praise Jesus. Lizzie really had a

ton of spit going there. I wish she'd just run off with a punk band already.

Henry is still fixated on the flowers. Henry tends to fixate.

"Anika, does that even work? Do you like the flowers? Or is it dumb?"

I dust myself off and take a seat between Henry and my mom.

"It works if you like the guy."

"And you do, right? You like the guy?" Henry tends to obsess.

"What?"

"You like the guy?"

"Which guy?"

"Uh, the guy who sent you flowers. Duh."

But I'm not here now. These flowers are here. And Henry is here. And Mom is here. And this note from Jared is here. But I'm not anywhere near here. I'm in a magical land of make-believe.

There's no reason for it, and it makes no sense, but all I can do is stare out the back window and wish that somehow Logan would appear. I wish he would appear and tell me how to take all the bad things out of him. But I can't. I can't erase all those slaps and bruises and God knows what else that his father gave him.

No one can. And the worst part is . . . none of that is Logan's fault. That bad piece of him. That bad piece got given to him like dirt-colored hair and alabaster skin.

So, you see, that makes me a horrible person—maybe even the worst person ever—for answering Henry's question, "Yeah. Of course I like him."

fifty-one

School is a completely different place now. Before it was something to endure. Something to not screw up. Not anymore. Now that I'm Jared Kline's girlfriend and everybody knows it, school has become like this place for me to go and be worshipped. It's kind of freaky.

It's still me over here. I'm still the same. But now everyone is acting like they better be nice to me or I'll have their heads chopped off. Seriously. Like one false move and I'll send them to walk the plank.

Jenny Schnittgrund invited me to go tanning with her. She has a free pass and was wondering if I could go, like, if I was into it.

Charlie Russell wants to know if I want to come out

to his family's ranch and go riding. They have a couple of horses and it's really fun, because the horses are really easy to ride. Maybe I could bring Jared . . . ?

And the pep squad girls are, basically, following me around like I have my own personal pep squad.

Give me an A! Give me an N! Give me an I-K-A!

What's that spell?!

ANIKA! ANIKA! GOOOOOO ANIKA!!

Not literally, of course. But seriously.

The only one normal is Shelli.

Shelli is the only person at this school who is acting exactly the same as she was before. Thank God. I couldn't take it if she started acting different. I think I'd have to give up on humanity entirely then—throw my hands in the air and ask God to hurry up with the Apocalypse already.

Becky keeps trying to elbow Shelli out of the way in order to be my new BFF. So far this morning she's offered to have me over after school, have a sleepover Friday, and go together to Chip Rider's Homecoming party, which is basically THE place to be for Homecoming. Never mind that I've only been to her house like twice, she's never even uttered the word *sleepover*, and usually is one of the hosts of that Homecoming party.

It's okay, Becky. I forgive you. It's not your fault you were born with the inner cortex of a velociraptor.

Yes, somehow the keys to the kingdom have landed on my lap and now the whole school is acting like I'm Princess Leia or something. Just to make sure I didn't wake up in a parallel universe, I duck into the bathroom, where Stacy Nolan is fixing her makeup. When she sees me she drops her lip liner in the sink.

"Is it true?!"

"Is what true?"

"That you're Jared Kline's girlfriend?"

"I think so."

"Whoa. That's crazy."

"I know, right?"

But now Becky and Shelli make their way in to find me, and Becky starts in on Stacy.

"Hey, Stacy, have any babies lately?"

Stacy looks at me for help.

"Um . . . she was never even pregnant. Remember?" That's the best I can do, on the fly.

But Becky's not letting this go. She's just sharpening her knives.

"Oh, right. Who would wanna fuck *her*?"

And now Stacy's gonna have to redo her eyeliner because her eyes are starting to well up. Shelli ducks out, not wanting to deal with any of this, and honestly, I wish I could duck out, too.

"Seriously? Like what's the point?" I ask.

And now Becky turns on me.

"What?!"

"I mean, what's the point? You got what you wanted, she's in tears now, I mean . . . just . . . can't you just leave it alone?"

"Wow. I guess someone's getting too big for her britches."

And I know it's coming. I know it is. Here it is.

"Immigrant." She says it like a curse.

Stacy's given up on her makeup now. Shelli's peeking in from the hall. This is not good.

"Look. All I'm saying is sometimes these things you say hurt people like a lot more than you think, okay?"

Ugh. That didn't come out right.

And now Becky looks at me. Her eyes turn into two little slits and I can tell she's plotting her attack. I'm so dead now. Stone-cold silence.

And then, out of nowhere, Becky lets out a laugh. But it's not a funny laugh and it's not a happy laugh. It's a laugh with daggers in it.

"Ha-ha! Ha-ha-ha! So you're like Mother Teresa now?"

She walks out of the bathroom, swiping Shelli out of the way, right before the bell.

fifty-two

I don't want Jared Kline to pick me up from school today even though that means I'm crazy because everybody worships him and he sent me the largest flower bouquet in history. I don't know what I want. But it's not to get driven out to God-knows-where and have him slobber all over me, apologize, and then ask if I'm a virgin, that's for sure.

There's an open patch in the chain link off the track field that some heshers ripped apart so they could go out and smoke during gym. After seventh period I make a beeline to the bathroom and duck out the back; not even Shelli sees me.

I can look out, by the side of the school, and see Jared in his trucker hat, parked in front. Becky and Shelli are standing there and everybody looks slightly confused. I know I'm supposed to be there. I know I am. That's the deal. But I just can't. I just don't want to be in that position. Like ever. Out in the middle of nowhere with nowhere to go and completely at the mercy of someone who, quite frankly, I don't trust, or do trust, or maybe trust a little.

Sure, last time he just jumped me and then turned around and gave me flowers but what's he gonna do next time? Rape me and then turn around and ask me to marry him? I mean, the guy's kinda like a loose cannon.

I know, I know. Without him I'm screwed. Now that Becky has it out for me, without Jared Kline I'm dead. Like, over. *Switch schools* over.

Even Shelli won't be able to save me. She'll have to save herself. And she will. I know it. I don't hold it against her or anything. All's fair in the mean streets of tenth grade.

Ducking out from behind the track field I feel a sense of exhilaration, even though I'm probably blowing it big-time. Something about leaving Jared, Becky, and everybody else just waiting there at the altar feels like that song John Lennon made with that Asian chick when he left the Beatles.

I'm about five blocks down the street toward my house, a different route than Shelli and I take 'cause right now I just wanna be alone. And this is when I hear it. Logan's moped. I'd know that sound in my sleep. He's coming past me fast and he stops at the curb and takes off his helmet.

We both just stand there looking at each other. There's a thousand miles in between us but also it's kind of like an electromagnetic field you could power a city with.

"Jared Kline, huh? I shoulda known."

"Look, Logan. I dunno . . ."

"Look. Just . . . here . . . I was gonna give this to you the other night . . . just take it."

He hands me a piece of paper, folded up into a triangle.

We catch eyes and it's like getting punched in the gut. Every single part of me wants to get on that moped with him and ride off into the sunset but that's like a world that doesn't exist anymore, with rainbows and unicorns and fairy dust.

He's just about to put on his helmet and ride off.

"Hey, wait."

He stops.

"How are you? How's your dad? How're your kid brothers?"

He looks at me like I might as well be wearing a dunce cap.

"You really wanna know?"

"Yeah."

"My dad's weird. Like really weird. My brothers are cute. And my mom's a drunk."

And with that he puts on his helmet and rides off over the hill, past the skinny freezing trees.

There's no way I can wait till I get home to read this. I open up the little triangle and inside, across the top: "A HAIKU." Then underneath is the haiku. Five-seven-five. This is what it says:

Ceaseless. Almost too
much for this small frame. You make
me part of the sky.

fifty-three

At dinner all I can do is think about Logan. I've got that crazily beautiful haiku playing over and over in my head on repeat. Ceaseless. Almost too much for this small frame. You make me part of the sky . . . Ceaseless. Almost too much for this small frame. You make me part of the sky . . . over and over again on repeat and everybody around me, Lizzie, Neener, Robby, Henry, Mom, the ogre, are just sitting there eating their mashed potatoes as if everything's great and the world is not ending and it's all I can do not to pick up the bowl of mashed potatoes and throw it across the room.

Jesus Christ.

Did I make the wrong decision did I make the wrong decision did I make the wrong decision?

Ceaseless.

Almost too much for this small frame.

You make me part of the sky.

Fuck!

It doesn't help that right smack dab in the middle of the table are those goddamn flowers.

My mom is the only one to notice that I'm basically going insane. She keeps trying to catch my eye and I keep avoiding it. She knows me. She can read my thoughts like a Jedi. But I avoid her. And after dinner, I avoid her some more. I duck into my room, where I take the piece of paper out and look at it again.

Here's the equation. Pure and simple. If I break up with Jared Kline I am dead. Dead to Becky. Dead to Shelli. Dead to Pound High and everybody in it. Becky will make my life worse than hell. She will make my life Oklahoma. She will go after me worse than Shelli, worse than Stacy Nolan, worse than Joel Soren.

If I stay with Jared Kline, even though I'm not sure if he's full of shit or the greatest thing ever, none of that will happen. I will rule the school for the rest of my career there and maybe even beyond.

The problem is Jared Kline may actually be the scam artist everyone says he is. A really good one who is just really, really convincing and then, once he convinces me to fall totally, completely, 100 percent in love with him and gets me to bone him, he'll dump me like an old bag of Fritos.

And then there's Logan.

Logan is a sideways, brilliant, honest guy who does the coolest stuff ever, and everybody hates, but who I am basically in love with.

But Logan is damaged, broken. And, let's not sugarcoat it, that ain't gonna change.

Even though it isn't his fault, even though his shitty father caused it, even though it's not fair . . . that kinda thing cuts deep. That kinda thing sticks.

Wouldn't a good person stick with *him*? Wouldn't a good person try to help somehow?

Dear Lord above tell me what to do tell me what to do tell me what to do.

Yes, I'm on my knees now, praying. Don't judge me and don't call me a weirdo. The fact is I need help and I need it fast because I feel like I'm gonna pull my hair out in pieces and tear my skin off my face.

I am such a shitty person. I'm an idiot.

I am lost.

Dear Lord above tell me what to do tell me what to do tell me what to do.

My mom is knocking on my door, has been knocking on my door, but I'm not hearing. Finally, she peeks in.

"Honey, your friend Jared's on the phone."

Oh God. Not now.

"Um, tell him . . . tell him I'm dead."

"Honey . . ."

"I dunno, Mom. Tell him I'm asleep or something."

"Anika, it's six o'clock."

"Mom, just make something up. Please?"

"Okay but . . . you wanna tell me what's wrong?"

"No, Mom. I'm just. I'm just . . . tired or something."

She looks at me and I can tell she wants to make it better. Just like every time she's made it better since I was born. Crying. Make it better. Colic. Make it better. Got a boo-boo. Make it better. Scraped my knee. Make it better. And there are a million things my mom could do, and has done, to make it better. But none of those things will reach up under my skin and make me a different person. None of those things will reach up under my skin and make me good.

fifty-four

The next day I wake up with a 103 temperature and my mom refuses to let me out of the house. Not that I put up much of a fight. The last thing I want to do is go to school today, or tomorrow, or ever again. Really all I want to do is fly up into the stars with Logan. But it's simple. I can't have what I want. That's it.

Well, it wouldn't be the first time in the history of mankind that a fifteen-year-old girl in the middle of nowhere didn't get what she wanted. I'm sure there are thousands of fifteen-year-old girls who had exactly the opposite of what they wanted. Like getting burned at the stake, for instance. Or getting married off to an eighty-year-old man in a trade for some sheep.

No, this is a "first world problem," as the vampire would say. The answer, he would say, is getting good grades.

The vampire must be reading my thoughts now because, as if on cue, he calls and demands to speak to me.

"I have spoken to your mother and she says you are sick, is dat true?"

"Yes, Dad. I'm sick."

"Is dat all?"

"Yeah."

"Dere is something wrong with you. Vhat is the matter?"

"I dunno, Dad, I'm just upset about something."

"Is it a boy?"

"Kinda."

"Are you pregnant? You are not allowed to get pregnant."

"No, Dad. God. No. I'm not, geez, how embarrassing."

"Okay, good, because dat vould ruin your life, you understand?"

"Yes, Dad."

"Is it interfering with your grades? You cannot let any of these een-significant dramas get in the vay of your grades. Dat is the most important, you understand?"

"Yes, I do."

"Are you sure?"

"Yes, Dad. My grades are fine. I'm even tutoring the other kids in computer programming."

"Dat is good. Although I'm not sure you vant to be a computer geek."

"Dad, where did you even learn that word?"

"Oh, come on. I do not live in the Dark Ages. Contrary to popular belief."

"Okay, Dad."

"If I think dere is any een-dication dat you are jeopardizing your future in that godforsaken place, I vill not hesitate to bring you back here to Princeton, vhere I have unlimited resources to educate you at the best private schools thees country has to offer. In fact, it may be more appropriate—"

"Dad. It's not hurting my grades. I promise."

"Even dat overinflated physical education instructor? Has he seen fit to give you an A? Or is he under the deluded impression that his meaningless little life vould be given gravitas by giving a tenth-grade, straight A student a B for not jumping rope to his liking?"

"No, I think I turned him around, Dad."

"Good. Okay, vell I have to catch a plane to Geneva. I am doing a conference dere. I vill send you a postcard."

"Okay, Dad."

"Remember. I have the means, here, to give you a first-rate education. If you ever decide you vant to leave dat horrible place, I vould be glad to assist you in dat endeavor. Plus, dere might be something to be said for having quality time vith your father before you die. Now, good-bye."

And with that, my father, the vampire, is off the phone and off to Switzerland. And then Prague, then maybe Leningrad. You'll never know where he is until you get the postcard. Spires and turrets and gargoyles staring down from somewhere in the middle of Europe and a note. "Anika, here is a picture of Vienna. I have a speaking engagement here. Big kiss, Père."

Père. That's French, for "Dad." That little French word is the closest we will ever get to affection.

My mom comes in after I hang up the phone to assess the damage. She knows, by now, that one phone call from the vampire can devastate me for days. If he chooses to turn that withering sense of humor on me. To eviscerate. Which is his skill set. The one thing about the vampire, stay on his good side. But don't try to get too close. If you do, he'll bite you.

My mom sits next to me on the bed.

"Everything alright?"

"Yeah."

"Did you know I got a letter for you?"

"What? When?"

"This morning. It's from Oakland. Do you know anybody from Oakland?"

"No, Mom. Definitely not."

"Honey, is there something you're not telling me?"

"No, Mom."

"Okay. Here it is. Now get back to bed, you need your rest."

And there it is, a letter from Oakland. Who the hell lives in Oakland? I've never even been west of Colorado.

I snuggle up in my sheets and open it.

It's from Tiffany.

> Dear Anika,
>
> Well, I made it! I'm in Oakland! With my grandma. She was super-happy to see me and her place is really nice, it's got two floors and everything. Please don't tell anybody where I am, especially my mom, okay? I just wanted to write to you and say thank you. If it wasn't for you I never would have made it here. I took the train. It was really pretty. We went through the mountains and it was crazy. You've never seen so much snow. I was kind of scared, a little. Like, if we got stuck we'd have to eat each other. Well, bye for now, I just wanted to say thanks.
>
> Your friend,
>
> Tiffany
>
> PS: I feel grateful to you for what you did but I have to admit, I still don't understand. Why would you take anything when you have

everything you need right there in front of you?

PPS: My grandma won't let me keep the money, she says it's bad luck, so here it is. I rounded up, so it wouldn't jingle in the mail.

And there, behind the letter: Exactly one thousand two hundred thirty-seven dollars. Goddamn it.

Even Tiffany all the way out there in Oakland knows better than me.

What do you think? Do you think I should keep her secret? Her mom's probably freaking out. I mean, it kind of seems like a girl belongs with her mom but . . . maybe not that mom, I guess. Anyway, anything's better than that shit-ass place down by the interstate.

Bullet point number two. What am I supposed to do with this money?

$1,237.00.

I could keep it and add it to my college fund. Do I even have a college fund?

My mom knocks on the door again.

"Honey, how are you feeling?"

"Mom."

"Yes."

"Do you wanna hear something stupid?"

"I guess, honey."

"I stole one thousand two hundred thirty-six dollars and fifty cents from the Bunza Hut and now I don't even want it."

Silence.

"What?"

"Mom. I'm a thief. I'm a horrible person and I know that you tried but I'm a thief and I stole all this money, also, I used to scrape up your Valium and put it in Mr. Baum's Folger's."

"What?!"

"So he wouldn't be so mean to Shelli. I mean he was, like, really mean to her."

"Honey, you can't just go around poisoning people!"

"I know. I know I'm a terrible person and I know I'm going to jail but could you please just forgive me because I did it for a good cause."

"You stole for a good cause?"

"Kinda."

"I'm not sure I'm following, honey. . . ."

"I gave it to Tiffany, after she got busted. But she gave it back to me. See. I'm a failure. Even as a Robin Hood–like character of redemption, I have failed."

"Honey . . . okay. I'm gonna close this door and we are gonna figure this out together, okay?"

"Okay."

fifty-five

My mom has me bundled up like a snowman and we are driving up Sheridan Boulevard to Mr. Baum's house. And by house I mean mansion. It's almost sunset and the sun is shining through the trees before making its final exit. I guess, for this, she can let me out of the house. With a 103 temperature. Where obviously I will catch pneumonia and die.

"Okay, you're gonna sit in the car, okay? Just stay put."

I nod.

My mother has suddenly become a spy in her own personal espionage thriller. Her tone is conspiratorial and, yes, she is wearing sunglasses and a trench coat.

It suddenly dawns on me.

Is my mom crazy?

Maybe all this time I was not the only freak in the family. Maybe the apple doesn't fall far from the tree. And maybe that tree is sitting right next to me in giant sunglasses and a trench coat.

"Okay, now. On the count of three I am gonna run up there, leave the drop, and then we'll make a break for it."

Drop.

We're gonna "leave the drop."

Then we're gonna "make a break for it."

Seriously. What is happening? Meanwhile, Frosty the Snowman over here is bundled up to complete immobility. She keeps telling me to stay in the car, completely unaware that I have absolutely no choice in the matter. I couldn't move if the dashboard caught fire.

"Okay. Ready now? One . . . two . . . THREE!"

She scurries out and over the snow, a trench-coated figure in a sea of white. The path up the driveway leads to a cobblestone walk to the front door. A grand affair with two giant wooden doors and a wrought-iron knocker.

She "makes the drop," turns around, and scurries back to the car.

Inside, a dog starts barking.

"Shit! Shit! Shit!"

She jumps in and suddenly we are peeling out backward

as the front porch light of Mr. Baum's mansion goes on and my mom speeds down Sheridan like she's Billy the Kid.

I sit bundled in my snowman outfit, unable to move or remark, for that matter. I mean, the whole thing is so ludicrous, but I'm kind of in awe of my mother at this point.

Also, I have now come to the happy conclusion that I get my "specialness" from her. Mystery solved!

Although, to be honest, I will miss that $1,237.00 included in "the drop."

My mom keeps looking suspiciously in the rearview mirror. I can practically hear her heart beating from here.

"Okay." She exhales. "I think we lost 'em."

fifty-six

Two days later and I'm still in bed with the flu or a cold or probably cholera. I'm lying back in bed now, bundled. My mom has the sheets up and is taking my temperature. She takes out the thermometer.

"Okay. Ninety-nine-point-three. That's better."

She puts the thermometer away and fluffs up the pillows.

"You still have to rest though, okay?"

"You mean like don't go on any weird heists where we 'make a break for it'?"

She smiles and tucks me under the blanket.

"Exactly."

"Mom?"

"Yes, honey."

"Do you think that maybe you have a future in the Secret Service?"

My mom laughs.

It's the dumbest thing in the world but I feel like a huge anvil has been taken off my shoulders ever since we burned rubber out of Mr. Baum's driveway.

"Mom, I think you saved the day, kinda."

"What do you mean, honey?"

"Well, like, I think that whole thing was really bothering me, like rotting my guts out or something."

"Oh yeah? So, lemme ask you a question, then. Was it actually worth the thousand dollars—"

"One thousand two hundred thirty-six dollars and fifty cents."

"Okay, was it worth that EXACT amount . . . to feel like that?"

"Mom, is this an after-school special?"

"No. No, it's not. But I wanna know. Was it worth it?"

Ugh. I hate it when anybody else is right.

"No, Mom, it wasn't. It was dumb."

"Okay, good. So now I don't have to worry about that anymore . . . ?"

"No. You don't."

"Good. 'Cause you could ruin your future. Then what

would your father do?"

"He'd probably go to Vienna. Oh, wait, he already did that."

"Just remember, no stealing. It's rude."

"Mom, wanna hear something stupid?"

"Please. No. I can't take another heist."

"I love you."

My mom looks down at me. She gets a little weepy, or maybe she's just tired. It's been three days of taking care of sicko me, not to mention the other four rapscallions around here.

"I love you, too, honey. Just stop poisoning people."

She kisses me on the forehead.

"Now go to sleep, little cubby."

She tucks me in and shuts the door behind her.

I can't seem to keep my head up with all this Tylenol and chicken soup she's plied me with. She's got me bundled up like an Eskimo with Vicks VapoRub slathered all over the place and a humidifier by the bed. My mom is not messing around when it comes to colds. Or flus.

The ceiling is starting to turn into oatmeal and I can't keep my eyes open even for a minute. Somehow the letter and the phone call and the haiku and the heist are all too much to think about and my head goes clunk on the pillow and suddenly I'm staring at that crystal white painting from Logan. Maybe, if I'm lucky, I'll wake up in Geneva or Zermatt or Vienna. Maybe I'll wave to the vampire and he'll wave back, if I'm getting straight As. If I flunk, he'll keep walking.

fifty-seven

In my dream I'm standing on a sheet of snow, stretched out in a basin underneath the mountains of Switzerland. Behind me is the Matterhorn and it's a bright blue sky, the color of a Tiffany box. It's me but in a way it's not me, standing there. Me in a white dress and everything is white white white. It's the most beautiful place I've ever been, like a charmed crystal forest, and on the other side, coming out of the black, is Logan. He's standing there, and even though he's miles away I can see him, see into his eyes.

We're getting moved toward each other, like the snow basin is a conveyor belt, moving us together and now we are closer, closer and now we are close. Now he is right in front of me and the sky is bright white and it starts to snow, just little pieces, little by little, snowflake by snowflake, and we both know that this is the most enchanted place in the world, this place between us. And he leans in and I lean in and it's a kiss, a chaste kiss, that becomes a not-so-chaste kiss and now it's like we are turning into, turning into one thing, turning into each other, turning into the white light and the snowflakes and we are light light light and just about to float up into the sky, up past the mountains and the black forest and the Matterhorn and up up up over the whole wide world.

But then the black forest trees turn spiky and spindly and mean, they reach out from behind Logan and grab him with their arms, pulling him back, and the white snow basin caves in and suddenly there is nothing, nothing underneath and the black blade trees take Logan down down down and away, away further. And I'm screaming, or I'm trying to scream but nothing's coming out and we're looking at each other, across the freezing ice abyss and we're helpless, helpless and no one can hear me, no one can see, and then I look to find him, I look everywhere around me and through the ice and the tree branches and the snow forest, but he's gone.

I wake up with a jump and now I'm covered with sweat and it's so quiet you can hear your breath and something's wrong. But nothing's wrong. It was just a dream. That was just a dream I had, but it was so real, it felt like more real even than this now. This here, that *is* real.

The clock is blinking: 4:13.

4:13.

4:13. And stone-cold silence. None of it was real, it was just a dream. Don't be silly.

But there's something weird. There's something tugging me out of bed and down the hall. Down the hall, which seems now longer than I remember it. And I'm walking. Like I'm sleep-walking but no, now I'm awake. I'm awake now. This is my house. This is my hallway. That is my phone.

And I pick up the phone.

What am I doing?

What the fuck am I doing?

Oh, I know what I'm doing. I'm gonna call Logan. I'm gonna call Logan now and tell him I'm in love with him.

And I know this now.

I know this like I know the sky is blue and I know the world is round and I know the moon revolves around the earth, the earth revolves around the sun. And I can't wait to tell him. I can't wait to tell him and it's gonna be just like that kiss, just like that kiss in the snow cloud and he and I are gonna be like light and air, together.

But it's 4:17. You can't call someone at 4:17. You can call

them at ten at night maybe, or maybe nine in the morning if it's urgent. But not 4:17. You can't do that. That's just weird. Nobody will be up even and then you'll just wake everybody. And what are you gonna say, "Put Logan on. 'Kay, thanks. Hey, Logan, I had a dream about a bunch of snow and I'm in love with you."

No, no. Wait for tomorrow. Wait for tomorrow and tell him after school. Or before school. Or at school? Who gives a shit anyways. Just tell him at school. You're gonna tell him. You're gonna tell him at school. And then it'll be you and him together.

fifty-eight

There's a TV on when I wake up, which is weird. It's about 5:00 a.m., which is weird. We're not a house that wakes up at five in the morning and we're certainly not a house that's got the TV on at five in the morning, my mom makes sure of that. The TV goes on at night, after schoolwork, and even then, just for a little bit. One show, maybe two. I mean, the ogre watches TV all night long after dinner, lets it put him to sleep every night. But not us. TV in the morning is not us.

But it's on.

And there's a commotion.

There's voices and whispers and shushing and then more and more of the TV.

I can hear Lizzie, and Neener. Henry just said something, and Robby, too. My mom shushing them. All of them up at five in the morning.

"Shush now. Shush up. Be quiet. Don't wake her."

Don't wake who?

Don't wake who? Don't wake me? It has to be me. I'm the only "her" in the house that is not awake.

I stand at the door and listen.

"Shush. Lizzie. I mean it."

I peek out and Lizzie's got her hand over her mouth. So does Neener. Robby is sitting down and Henry looks pale as a ghost. Henry looks like someone just sucked all his blood out and replaced it with ice water.

"You gotta tell her, Mom."

And now I can't take it.

"What? Tell me what?"

And I'm rushing into the room toward the TV and they're parting between them, everyone but my mom, who tries to get in my way. In the background, the TV blares. It's a voice, an excited voice. It's a news voice. It's someone on the news.

"Honey, listen, I think we should talk about this—"

But I'm past her. I'm past Mom and I'm past Lizzie and Neener and Henry and Robby. I'm past all of them and in front of the TV, in front of the happy blonde hairstyle and sad news face and concerned, excited words coming out of the newscaster.

And she's in front of something, too. The newscaster. She's in front of something with sirens and cars and lights swirling.

She's in front of Logan's.

fifty-nine

Pedaling fast fast fast, this is the moment. One of those movie moments you never think is gonna happen to you, but then it happens to you, and now it's here.

Pedaling fast fast fast, this is my only chance to stop it. This is the place where it looks like everything is gonna go horribly wrong and there's no hope, but then because it's a movie there is hope after all and there is a surprise that changes everything and everyone breathes a sigh of relief and everybody gets to go home and feel good about themselves and maybe fall asleep in the car.

Pedaling fast fast fast, this is the moment, this is the moment I get to remember for the rest of my nights and my days and my looking at the ceiling. Over that hill and down the next, through those trees and past the school.

Pedaling fast fast fast, this is the moment, by the time I get there you can see the lights going blue, red, white, blue, red, white, blue, red, white, little circles diced up in sirens and you think you can stop it but of course you can't, how could you ever think you could?

Pedaling fast fast fast, this is the moment.

This is the moment, and it's too late.

sixty

By the time I skid my bike to a stop the whole town's on Logan's street. The neighbors, the cops, the ambulances, everywhere there's ambulances and everywhere there's doctors and EMTs and IVs and bodies. There's bodies.

There's bodies on the stretchers.

One of the stretchers is going one way, in a hurry, surrounded by EMTs and IVs and orders being barked. The other stretchers are going in the other direction, more slowly, there's nothing there. No urgency. Nothing.

On the first stretcher, swarming with EMTs, there's a little sock. A little sock coming out with R2-D2. There's a little sock coming out and I know that sock because that's Billy's sock and he was wearing that sock the night Logan put him to bed and now that sock is soaked with blood and I can see it out of the blanket. Now that sock is soaked in blood now that stretcher is getting put in that ambulance and I'm not the only one seeing that sock and everyone, everyone has their hands to their mouths because everybody is seeing that sock.

And behind that stretcher, glued to that stretcher, are Logan's mom and Logan's kid brother, still in his camouflage sleeper. And his mom and his brother are hurrying in, hurrying in behind, glued to that stretcher, being carried away, too, lights swirling round and round, fast enough. It's gone, it's gone. That means hope. There's hope for that stretcher.

And now there's a second stretcher. God, please stop pulling out stretchers from that house but no one is listening no one is listening and here comes another one.

This one is big. A big body, a big, big body and something silent here. And that sheet is coming all the way up. And that stretcher is going slow. But that's two, that's two stretchers coming out from that house and that's enough Lord, please Lord, make that enough but it's not enough it's not enough and now the front door opens and it's one more.

The front door opens and it's one more.

And there is that hand. And there are those feet. And that is the hand that tucked in those R2-D2 socks under those *Star Wars* sheets. That is the hand that tucked in that Spider-Man sleeper. That is the hand that reached out to me and pulled me next to him and flew me past the trees on his moped. That is the hand that I dreamed about last night. That is the hand on that body that was supposed to be next to me, on that body that I fell in love with and that head and that heart, too. That is the hand and it's not moving.

It's not moving.

sixty-one

They're trying to grab me now. My mom and these people, some of them are in their bathrobes. They're trying to grab me and hold me back and get me out of here. They're trying to stop me from getting through this police tape. They're trying to stop me. But they can't stop me because no one can stop me because that's Logan. That's Logan over there on that stretcher and that stretcher is covered in blood and that stretcher is moving away, away but it can't go away, you can't take him away, please don't take him away, we were supposed to be together. And I'm on my knees now and my mom and these people, who are all these people, have me by the shoulders but I'm almost to Logan. I'm almost to Logan. I can touch him. I can touch him and bring him back to life.

I can bring him back to life I can just let me near him.

But they've got me and my mom's voice is coming out of somewhere, I can hear her:

"No, no, Anika. No, Anika, please, just, please, honey, I'm here. I'm here. I've got you. I'm here."

And the stretcher is gone the stretcher is moved past me. The stretcher is going away away and in that door and in that ambulance and that door closes and all is quiet, everything is quiet now, and everything is swirling now and the ambulances and light swirl round and round above me and there's a voice and a body holding me and there's a voice and a body keeping me from turning into a trillion tiny pieces and falling into the ground.

"I'm here. I'm here, honey. It's okay. I've got you."

sixty-two

This is the official report in the *Lincoln Journal Star*:

A Lincoln man distraught over his debts attempted to kill his wife and three children. The wife and two youngest sons survived and were found on the back stairwell of the house at approximately 4:45 a.m. The oldest son and father were killed in the altercation. The police were called after neighbors reported shots fired. The two bodies were found, dead on arrival, on the front landing. The injured son was rushed to the hospital in critical condition. He is now stable after being wounded by a stray bullet. The incident occurred in the Lincoln southeast suburb shortly after 4:00 a.m. A suicide note left open was found on the kitchen counter. In it, forty-two-year-old Steven McDonough expressed remorse about his overwhelming debts and "clearly indicated he was sorry he had to take the lives of his wife and children," Police Chief Meier reported. The victim was identified as fifteen-year-old Logan McDonough. It is believed he died in an attempt to save the lives of his mother and younger brothers. The father, Steven McDonough, reportedly had a blood-alcohol level of 0.25% when found. The mother and two surviving sons are recovering and receiving both medical and psychiatric treatment after the incident. All condolences, donations, and cards may be sent to St. Mary's Community Hospital, where a fund for the family is being organized.

It doesn't say: "Yeah, that would explain why Logan's dad was always spending tons of money and then acting really weird."

It doesn't say: "Yeah, you know, Logan's dad was actually a total gun freak who had a fucking arsenal of guns and ammo in his basement. Enough to hold off an army of zombies for two weeks straight and maybe that's not such a good idea when the guy's obviously got a screw loose."

It doesn't say: "Yeah, that makes sense why Logan's mom was a raging alcoholic because you gotta figure that guy was not a good guy to spend your life with."

It doesn't say: "Thank God there were two sets of steps in that house so that the mother and those two little boys could hide while Logan thwarted his batshit dad and basically gave his life protecting them as he'd probably done a million times, a million ways before."

It doesn't say: "Oh, by the way, I was in love with Logan and now I'll never be able to tell him and he died not even knowing that and why the fuck should he have died anyway, just 'cause his dad was a paranoid gun-nut freak?"

But I know why he died, he died to save his mom and his kid brothers, and that's not fair either.

It doesn't say: "Logan's kid brothers looked like little angels in *Star Wars* pajamas and that fucking fuckface tried to shoot them dead, and what's the point in God, or anything in the universe, after that?"

It doesn't say: "God. Where the fuck were you last night?"

sixty-three

I guess my family is really worried about me because my sisters are both camped out in my room, which is weird considering how much they hate me. They're both just lying there, on their beanbags, camped in the corner of my room while I sleep and stare at the ceiling and don't talk to anyone.

It's sorta like even though they wrestle me and spit on me and torment me every chance they get, they know this is the kind of thing that might set me off, finally, and all the marbles will be lost, once and for all, and I will inevitably be carted off in a little white van with guys in white jackets because we all knew that was coming anyway.

Mr. Baum calls from the Bunza Hut and my mom says I

can't make it. She says to stop putting me on the schedule for a little while, which is my mom's way of saying I'm quitting. She never asked me about it or anything. She just knows. And she's right. It goes without saying that the Bunza Hut and I have parted ways.

Lizzie is just sitting there, reading some book about this guy Darcy and how everybody thinks he's a dick but then he turns out to be super-fantastic. Neener is painting her nails. Robby's at football practice, as usual. You could set your clocks by that. But he came in last night and gave me his lucky trophy. Now, that's something. That thing is usually in a glass case on lockdown. Every once in a while, Henry pokes his head in. He doesn't say anything, he just looks at my sisters, nods, goes away. Except this morning, he did have something to say, which is absolute Henry.

"They say they're gonna get all that life insurance. 'Cause it wasn't a suicide."

Lizzie and Neener look up at him, puzzling.

"Now they're rich."

We accept this news in silence.

My mom would be sleeping in the bed next to me, if she could, but she sees my sisters have taken a keen interest in my well-being, so she's allowing that miracle to transpire.

Jared calls a couple of times but Lizzie just hangs up on him.

Neener keeps bringing trashy magazines for me to take my mind off it, which is nice.

I really never would have thought my sisters would be so protective of me. Lizzie hasn't spat in my mouth once.

The ogre tried to peek in but my sisters diverted that little plan.

My sisters aren't having it. After years of seeing him dote on Robby, make airplanes with Henry, smile at Neener, tolerate Lizzie, but turn around and every time, every single time, grumble or grouse or disagree with anything and everything I say, including the sky is blue or the world is round . . . my sisters are not having it today.

The ogre does not get halfway down the hall.

You gotta hand it to Lizzie. Intimidation is her forte.

And Neener just gives me a nod.

"It's okay, kid. We got this one."

And then there's school. Tomorrow's the first day back and everybody's talking about how there's gonna be a memorial service in the gym. I can picture it now. Becky lives across the street. She'll make it into the Becky tragedy hour. She's probably got the eulogy written and she'll be crying, talking about her *best friend Logan* and how she's devastated, how she can't go on without him.

She probably has a whole season picked out in black.

sixty-four

I don't know why but the ogre is driving me to school today. I am not happy about it. He doesn't say anything the whole time and neither do I. I'm not gonna say anything if he's not. No way.

We pull up to the curb and I'm about to hop out and get this excruciating drive over with but he stops me.

Ugh.

"Anika. I just want to say something."

"Um. Okay . . ."

"I know you don't like me. And I know you think I don't like you."

"Actually, I know you don't like me so—"

"Maybe I just don't know what to say to you!"

That was weird. Kind of came out of left field.

"I'm a middle-aged man who works all day to keep food on the table for five teenagers."

"Okay."

"And I may not be some smooth operator like your dad but I'm here. And I'm doing the work. And I love your mom. And I love you kids. And yeah, that means you, too."

"Um."

"And I'm really sorry about what happened to your friend."

It's probably because I'm tired but for some dumb reason this whole speech-at-the-curb thing is making me sort of misty. I mean, I don't even know where to start.

"And I'll try to think of something to say but, honestly, I don't have much in common with a fifteen-year-old girl. You know?"

"Well, maybe you could just start with 'hi' or something."

He nods.

"I love you kids and your mom very much. You're all I got."

I guess maybe this whole family-massacre incident has got to him because I could swear he's getting like choked up a little. Right here in the car.

"Alright. Um. We got a deal, I guess."

He looks up now. Still wispy but a little smile.

And with that I turn to go into the school. Well, I sure wasn't expecting that this morning. I mean, that was the last thing I ever thought was gonna happen. You know what I thought, actually? I thought my mom told him about the money and he was gonna ground me till college.

sixty-five

Everybody in the gym is dressed in black or wearing black armbands and there's a giant picture of Logan in the back, surrounded by white lilies. There's a big memorial wall and people have put down candles and flowers and written all sorts of shit like "Taken too soon" and "God be with you" and "We miss you." There sure are a lot of kind words for someone who, just two days ago, was considered a social pariah.

But everyone wants a part of this.

They want a part of the drama. They want a piece of it. They want to somehow seem meaningful by being closer to it. They were Logan's chemistry partner, they were in Logan's study group, they were Logan's friend.

Right now one of the teachers is up there, a pencil-thin woman in a black woolen skirt, just about to introduce a "very special speaker" and would that "very special speaker" come up to the podium.

And that "very special speaker" is Becky.

Of course.

Because Becky lived right across the street.

Shelli and I sit, side by side, in the front row, while Becky makes her way to the podium. All in black, she is the picture of teenage mourning. Her dress is Gucci. Freshly pressed. She dabs her eyes. She looks at the audience. She dabs her eyes again.

Some show.

She lets out a long sigh and begins . . .

"Logan McDonough was my neighbor. My classmate. My friend. Not many people knew about our strong bond, for it was something precious. More precious than idle gossip. It was so special; he was so special. Not very many people had the opportunity, like I did, to get to see Logan's inner heart, his brilliant thoughts, the way he would see the world in his own amazing, original way. And now . . ."

Pause.

Tears.

"And now that heart is snuffed out. Taken before its time."

More tears.

Tears enough to float a boat. Tears enough to make the teacher offer to rescue her. But, no! Becky holds up her hand. Becky is strong. Becky can do it. Becky is brave.

"But the truth is, Logan's heart will persevere. His heart will shine. Forever. Logan, you are eternal now. . . . I love you, Logan. We all do. We will miss you so."

Not a dry eye in the house.

Everyone is eating it up. It's like the whole school has amnesia.

The teacher gets up again. She is going to introduce the next "very special speaker" and that next "very special speaker" is me.

There's a silence, a few coughs, and shifting in seats as I reach the podium. Yes, I'm wearing black, too. But I look more like I just crawled out of the laundry machine.

I stand at the podium and look out at my classmates. It's gotta be about three hundred people. The whole school's in here. All that Pound High School has to offer. Even the heshers, somewhere in the back, by the bleachers. I have an entire speech written about Logan. About who he was and how brilliant he was and how there will never be anyone like him and how he was a real-life hero. Everyone is looking up at me and the teacher nods, an affirming nod. She's trying to tell me I can do it. I can do it. And to hurry up and get to it.

Silence.

And now I look out at the three hundred faces.

"Um. So. I was in love with Logan McDonough. He was my boyfriend."

There's a rustle and a few looks.

"He made two fake fire drills and left a painting for me in the middle of my art class."

In the back, I swear I can hear one of the heshers: "I knew it!"

I smile to myself, all that seems so far away now. . . .

"The second fake fire drill he filled the room with butterflies."

I catch Stoner Art Teacher's eyes and he nods and I know it's okay. He knows the truth, I know the truth, and he doesn't care. He even looks kind of moved.

"Logan was a misfit and a weirdo and it was like he was made of kryptonite. None of us wanted to touch him. But he wrote me the coolest haiku ever. It was the last thing he gave to me."

Everyone's leaning in, including Becky, and Shelli, and even the jocks. I take it out and try to hold my hand steady, but I know what it says.

"Ceaseless.

"Almost too much for this small frame.

"You make me part of the sky."

There's a silence in the auditorium. "It was kind of a secret. Actually. I kept it a secret. 'Cause I cared, I cared what everybody thought more than what I thought. Or more than my heart thought. And that makes me an idiot."

And now I look down at Becky looking at me, straight off the set of some soap opera scene she's made up in her mind. A scene where she is obviously the star and we are all just pointless extras. She actually looks annoyed that I'm stealing her thunder.

I could cry my face off right now but something else takes over, some rush of something rugged. Something sick of being soft.

I look at Becky for a long time.

"But now that I'm being honest, Logan McDonough thought Becky Vilhauer was a cunt. And so do I."

Shock.

Awe.

Christians are marrying Romans in the aisles.

Hatfields are making out with McCoys.

"Logan would have laughed his face off to hear that stupid Becky speech, which is the biggest piece of bullshit I've ever heard."

The teacher is looking at me like it's time to get off the mike, but that's not happening.

"Becky just makes shit up. Like how Stacy Nolan was pregnant. That was her. She just made it up. For fun. For her own personal amusement. Just for a laugh!"

I can see Stacy in the audience, turning bright red, and everyone is scuffling and turning in their seats and not knowing what to do with themselves because Santa Claus and the Easter Bunny and Jesus Christ might as well pop up behind me.

"She tortured poor Joel Soren on a constant basis. Just because one day he wouldn't give her a piece of bubble gum. Bubble gum! And now he gets beat up, every day. Tortured. All because of a dumb piece of Hubba Bubba."

I catch Jared in the back of the room. He gives me nod and a half grin. What is he doing here?

"Oh, and let's not forget she tried to fuck her boyfriend's older brother. Yes, Brad. Becky threw herself at your brother Jared, at your birthday party. How do I know? Because I was supposed to keep watch for 'the puppy dog.' That's what she called you."

I wish you could see Shelli's eyes.

And Becky—Becky is about to bum-rush the stage.

"And, finally, while we are on the topic of Jared Kline. Yes, I dropped Logan for Jared Kline because, well, for a whole bunch of reasons but one of them was that Logan wasn't cool. Because I *cared* that everybody thought Logan was a freak. That's something I'm going to have to live with for the rest of my life and, yes, it totally sucks and I'd do anything, anything in the world, to get him back. But just to be clear. Just to really put it all on the table . . . *Becky warned me that if I didn't drop that 'loser,' meaning Logan, I was done for.* So . . . so much for Becky's 'special relationship' with Logan. She's full of shit and Logan was way too good for her and, quite frankly, he was way too good for me, or any of us."

Becky is looking at me like my throat may as well already be slit.

"But here's the thing. Why are we all just acting like idiots and caring what stupidface Becky says about this or what so-and-so says about that? None of it matters. Right? I mean, does it really fucking matter?! Like, when you're eighty years old and on your deathbed do you really think it's gonna make you feel good to know you snickered at the right moment? At whatever thing or outfit or person that, according to Becky Vilhauer, wasn't cool? And what if you're like Logan? What if it all gets taken away, like that, one night out of nowhere? Do you really think any of this bullshit is going to matter? Do you? I mean, what the fuck is wrong with us?!"

Suddenly I realize I might as well be talking to a slab of concrete.

"Thank you and good night!"

Silence.

Crickets.

I look out into a sea of catatonic faces and realize it's over for me. It's over for me and that's that. I'm going to have to live with the vampire and go to private school back east after all.

Except.

In the back of the hall, I can hear it. A clap. One little clap. And it's Jared Kline. And then Brad stands up. A clap. And then another. Stacy Nolan stands up. One clap. And then another. And then Chip Rider. And then another. And then Jenny Schnittgrund. And then Joel Soren. And then Charlie Russell. And then, the heshers in the back. And suddenly, the whole auditorium is burst out into applause and—

And Becky is looking at Shelli, who is not standing. Shelli is sitting next to Becky like a bag of frozen peas. She looks at me. She looks at Becky. She looks at the entire auditorium full of jocks and brains and heshers and cheerleaders and back at me. And Becky is clinging to her, clinging to her arm like it's the last deck chair on the *Titanic*.

And Shelli stands up.

Shelli stands up and starts clapping.

And Becky melts into the ground. She melts sideways, like the Wicked Witch of the West, and scuttles out the auditorium door to the side like a wraith caught in daylight, and this makes everyone clap harder and for once in its life, Pound High is liberated from the great reign of Becky the Terrible and suddenly we are all together, emancipated, we are all free.

And I get to walk out the door now, walk right out through the middle with my head high, and I don't have to move away or jump off a bridge or anything. I get to walk down through that crowd, right past Jared Kline, who does the best thing ever because I guess Jared Kline always does the best thing ever, which is . . . he smiles and tips his trucker cap, like I was the greatest show on earth.

And I know, right there in that moment, that it's up to me now, that it was always up to me, and who knows maybe someday . . .

But not now because now I am out through the front doors and outside to the green grass field spread out in front of me like a magic carpet.

And walking across that field, hearing everyone behind me, getting quieter and quieter and further and further away, I make a promise up to the sky, up to Logan and beyond.

I won't forget. I won't forget you. I won't let them forget you. I don't know how, I don't even know when or how it could even be possible . . . but one day, I'll tell everyone about you, and you and me, and what happened and somehow I'll get to tell the whole world about you and how you wrote the most beautiful haiku in the world and I'll make it up to you, somehow, somehow, I'll make it up to you, I promise. And I think about them, too, the R2-D2 socks and Spider-Man sleeper, how Logan had to tell Billy his ankylosaurus had to stay at the foot of the bed to protect him.

And I want to throw my arms around Logan for what he did. I want to spin time backward and hold him close, close, and never let go. But that would be like grabbing the light out of the sunset and begging it not to leave the dusk.

And if I could, I would do every second of every moment over again if I knew the secret.

You get one chance.

You get to do this thing one time and you don't even know when it goes from swirling forward and around and around in circles to just a plain cold stop and nothing more. Can you believe it? All this time I've spent weighing this and weighing that, worrying about this and worrying about that, living back then and living forward, caring about what so-and-so thinks and about so-and-so, too, but never living here, *here*, this moment here. Never even acknowledging that this moment even exists, and it hits me, like a live volt through the chest.

This moment here.

This is all you get.

Before you are part of the sky.

acknowledgments

For Dylan McCullough, his brothers and his mother.

There have been so many noble and kind people I wish to thank for helping me along the way. My mother, Nancy Portes Kuhnel, and my best friend, Brad Kluck, first and foremost. Also, my astute agent, Josie Freedman, at ICM. Of course, my literary agent, Katie Shea Boutillier, at Donald Maas Literary Agency. And my incredible editor, Kristen Pettit, at HarperCollins, as well as the entire Harper team, especially Jennifer Steinbach Klonsky and Elizabeth Lynch. I have been lucky to have great editors along the way: Dan Smetanka for *Bury This*. Fred Ramey for *Hick*. My family: my brother, Charles De Portes, and my sister, Lisa Portes. My father, Dr. Alejandro Portes. My amazing steps: Maria Patricia Fernandez-Kelly, Doug Kuhnel, Nancy Kuhnel, and Bobby Kuhnel. Also, the people who made *Hick* such an amazing experience: Derick Martini, Chloë Grace Moretz, Eddie Redmayne, Teri and Trevor Moretz, Christian Taylor. Matthew Specktor, Joel Silverman, Dawn Cody, Noelle Hale, Stuart Gibson, Trevor Kaufman, John Limpert, Mira Crisp, Io Perry. Of course, my brilliant and kind fiancé, Sandy Tolan. And last but not least, the sun in my sky, the zing in my shoe-step, the most adorable little prince, my son, Wyatt Storm.